WITHDRAWN

✓ **W9-ATY-365**

A Young Jedi Faces the Dark Side Within Himself!

Suddenly the tubular transport started to vibrate furiously. Then it slowed to a dead stop halfway up the elevator shaft. The power had failed. Luke Skywalker and the twelve-year-old Jedi Prince were trapped in the darkness.

"Uh-oh," Ken said despondently. "Looks like we're history."

"Aren't you forgetting something, Ken?" Luke asked, putting a hand on the young Jedi Prince's shoulder.

"Like what?"

"The Force. With trust in the Force, we can do *anything*," Luke said. "Even move tons of solid steel. Once I watched Yoda use the Force to lift my spaceship out of the swamps of Dagobah—it floated, weightless, until he set it down. The Force is a Jedi's strength, Ken. The Force is the power that flows through all things, the power behind the light of the stars—"

PROPHETS OF THE DARK SIDE

STAR WARS®

The Adventure Continues . . .

titles in Large-Print Editions:

STAR WARS®

Book 6

PROPHETS OF THE DARK SIDE

PAUL DAVIDS
AND HOLLACE DAVIDS

Pencils by June Brigman
Finished Art by Karl Kesel

Gareth Stevens Publishing
MILWAUKEE

15.93

For a free color catalog describing Gareth Stevens' list of high-quality books and multimedia programs, call 1-800-542-2595 (USA) or 1-800-461-9120 (Canada). Gareth Stevens Publishing's Fax: (414) 225-0377.
See our catalog, too, on the World Wide Web: http://gsinc.com

Library of Congress Cataloging-in-Publication Data

Davids, Paul.
    Prophets of the Dark Side / Paul Davids and Hollace Davids.
        p. cm. — (Star wars)
        Summary: Having tempted the young Jedi Prince Ken into revealing the location of the Lost City of the Jedi, the Supreme Imperial Prophet Kadann plans to steal ancient knowledge and rule over a new tyrannical empire.
        ISBN 0-8368-1994-2 (lib. bdg.)
        [1. Science fiction.] I. Davids, Hollace. II. Title. III. Series: Davids, Paul. Star wars.
    PZ7.D282355Pr 1997
    [Fic]—dc21   97-21436

This edition first published in 1997 by
Gareth Stevens Publishing
1555 North RiverCenter Drive, Suite 201
Milwaukee, Wisconsin 53212 USA

Cover art by Drew Struzan
Interior pencils by June Brigman
Finished interior art by Karl Kesel

Printed in the United States of America

1 2 3 4 5 6 7 8 9 01 00 99 98 97

HPY

To Forrest J. Ackerman (Mr. Sci-Fi),
creator and editor of *Famous Monsters of Filmland* magazine. Thanks for raising us on such a robust diet of primordial beasts and automated robots so we were ready to fasten our space belts when George Lucas pointed the way to the stars.

Acknowledgments

With thanks to George Lucas, the creator of Star Wars, to Lucy Wilson for her devoted guidance, to Charles Kochman for his unfailing insight, and to West End Games for their wonderful Star Wars sourcebooks— also to Betsy Gould, Peter Miller, and Richard A. Rosen for their advice and help.

The Rebel Alliance

Luke Skywalker

Princess Leia

Han Solo

Chewbacca

Ken

Dee-Jay (DJ-88)

See-Threepio (C-3PO)

Artoo-Detoo (R2-D2)

The Empire

Trioculus

Grand Moff Hissa

Zorba the Hutt

Grand Moff Muzzer

Supreme Prophet Kadann

High Prophet Jedgar

Defeen

Triclops

A long time ago,
in a galaxy
far, far away...

The Adventure Continues . . .

It was an era of darkness, a time when the evil Empire ruled the galaxy. Fear and terror spread across every planet and moon as the Empire tried to crush all who resisted—but still the Rebel Alliance survived.

The headquarters of the Alliance Senate are located in a cluster of ancient temples hidden within the rain forest on the fourth moon of Yavin. It was the senate that now led the valiant fight to establish a new galactic government, and to restore freedom and justice to the galaxy. In pursuit of this quest, Mon Mothma, the Rebel Alliance leader, organized the Senate Planetary Intelligence Network, also known as SPIN.

SPIN conducts its perilous missions with the help of Luke Skywalker and his pair of droids known as See-Threepio (C-3PO) and Artoo-Detoo (R2-D2). Other members of SPIN include the beautiful Princess Leia Organa; Han Solo, the dashing pilot of the spaceship *Millennium Falcon*; Han's copilot Chewbacca, a hairy alien Wookiee; and Lando Calrissian, the former governor of Cloud City on the planet Bespin.

Lando now runs a space theme park known as Hologram Fun World. He had been forced to abandon his post as Governor of Cloud City after gambling away his position to Zorba the Hutt, a sluglike alien who is the father of the deceased gangster Jabba the Hutt.

Luke Skywalker and his twin sister Princess Leia follow the path of the Jedi. The Jedi Knights, an ancient society of brave and noble warriors, believed that victory comes not just from physical strength but from a mysterious power called the Force. The Force lies hidden deep within all things. It has two sides, one side that can be used for good, the other side a power of absolute evil.

Guided by the Force, and by the spirit of his first Jedi teacher, Obi-Wan Kenobi, Luke Skywalker was led to the legendary Lost City of the Jedi. Deep underground on the fourth moon of Yavin, the Lost City proved to be the home of a twelve-year-old boy named Ken, said to be a Jedi Prince. Ken had no human friends and had never before left the Lost City to journey aboveground. He knew nothing of his origins—only that he had been brought to the Lost City by a Jedi Knight in a brown robe—and had been raised from early childhood by a loyal group of caretaker droids who had once served the ancient Jedi Knights. Ken has since left the underground city and joined Luke and the Rebel Alliance.

With the Empire's evil leaders, Emperor Palpatine and Darth Vader, now destroyed, a new era has begun. A bitter feud developed between Kadann, the Supreme Prophet of the Dark Side, and Trioculus, a three-eyed tyrant who was formerly Supreme

Slavelord of the spice mines of the planet Kessel.

An impostor, Trioculus falsely claimed to be Emperor Palpatine's son. With help from Kadann and the Imperial grand moffs, Trioculus was aided in his rise to power so they could all share the rule of the Empire. Trioculus eventually failed in his rule and Kadann wrested control of the Empire for himself, although the grand moffs remained loyal to Trioculus.

The evil Emperor Palpatine did have a three-eyed son—Triclops, whose existence was kept secret. For most of Triclops's life, he remained a prisoner of the Empire, locked away in Imperial insane asylums. Eventually he escaped from the Imperial Reprogramming Institute on the planet Duro and denounced his father's Empire. After being discovered by Luke Skywalker, Ken, and Han Solo, he took refuge with the Rebel Alliance.

While Trioculus and the grand moffs were feuding with Kadann, they also had a dispute with Zorba the Hutt. Trioculus eventually defeated Zorba by tossing the old Hutt into the Mouth of Sarlacc at the Great Pit of Carkoon on Tatooine, expecting to be rid of him at last. But still Zorba survived when the Sarlacc spit him out, unable to digest the slimy Hutt's sluglike body.

Having also captured Princess Leia, Trioculus tried to turn her to the Dark Side, wanting to marry her and make her the Queen of the Empire. However, his plans were thwarted by a clever Alliance plan and a new Rebel weapon—the Human Replica Droid, which was a lifelike droid built to resemble the Princess. It fired lasers from its eyes, striking Trioculus in the chest and wounding him.

Safely rescued from the Imperial Moffship, Princess Leia and Han Solo intend to resume their wedding plans, but not by eloping at Hologram Fun World as they attempted before. Instead, it will be a formal ceremony at the Alliance Senate. Everything should proceed according to plan—as long as they steer clear of the ruthless tyranny of Supreme Prophet Kadann and his Prophets of the Dark Side!

CHAPTER 1
The Final Hour

Grand Moff Hissa steered across the security observation room inside the Imperial Moffship, riding his hover-chair on a cushion of air. He swiftly approached the motionless body that was lying on the floor. Hissa, who had accidentally lost his arms and legs in a pool of toxic waste on the planet Duro, could hear the sounds of shouts and scuffling coming from the corridor on the other side of the locked door. Imperial officers were growing anxious and quarrelsome, as rumors about the fate of Trioculus, their three-eyed leader, spread throughout the spaceship.

Trioculus, who was mortally wounded but still alive, reached up from where he lay, grasping onto one of Hissa's artificial metallic arms. Those arms had been taken from an Imperial assassin droid and fastened to the stumps at Hissa's shoulders. It had proven impossible for the medical droids to attach artificial legs at the grand moff's corroded hipbone; therefore he would be confined to the hover-chair for the rest of his days.

"Hissa," Trioculus groaned, "those foul Rebels have assassinated me—I'm dying."

Cold sweat dripped down Grand Moff Hissa's

neck as he stared in shock at Trioculus's horrible wounds. "This is a black day for the Empire, my Dark Lordship," Hissa said.

Grand Moff Hissa glanced away, noticing the remains of the Rebel Alliance's secret weapon. The weapon, known as a Human Replica Droid, was a robot so lifelike that it had actually fooled Trioculus and Grand Moff Hissa into thinking it was the real Princess Leia. The grand moffs had stared in shock as fiery green laser rays burst from the Human Replica Droid's eyes, striking Trioculus at close range.

Now the droid's smoldering remains lay crumpled on the chamber floor, incinerated by blasts from Imperial laser pistols. Grand Moff Hissa grimaced as he inhaled. The room was filled with the scent of burned synthetic flesh and smoking scorched hair, mixed with the foul odor of melted droid micro-circuits.

"Hissa," Trioculus gasped, "when I am gone, beware of Kadann. He will turn on you next, because you remained loyal to me until my death, rather than to him." Trioculus spoke slowly in a strained, rasping voice. "He will use his authority as Supreme Prophet of the Dark Side . . . to oppose you with all his power and strength."

"Let him oppose us, then," Hissa said, nodding. "We'll fight back, even if it means an all-out civil war for the Empire. That black-bearded dwarf has proven to be even more of a scoundrel than Zorba the Hutt."

"Zorba, yes . . . we dropped Zorba into the Great Pit of Carkoon," Trioculus recalled in a weakening voice, "sent him plunging into the hungry Mouth of Sarlacc—a fitting end for that slimy slug. Curse him!"

"And curse Kadann and his Prophets of the Dark Side," Grand Moff Hissa added.

"Yes," Trioculus agreed. "But let the darkest curse of all . . . fall upon Luke Skywalker. Promise me that . . . that you grand moffs," Trioculus struggled to speak, as the gasps between his words grew louder, ". . . that you will destroy that Jedi Knight once and for all." Trioculus's three eyes blinked and then half closed, as though staring off into the distance.

"It shall be done," Grand Moff Hissa said.

And then Trioculus exhaled, closing his three eyes for the last time.

A chill swept through the gray, dark room. For a frozen, shuddering moment, all was silent.

In a ceremony held before the officers and crew of the Moffship, the grand moffs placed Trioculus's lifeless body into a cremation chamber.

The fires of the chamber raged. When all that was left of Trioculus was a small pile of ashes, the grand moffs put equal amounts of his remains into four small canisters.

Four Imperial missile probes were prepared, each probe containing one of the canisters of Trioculus's ashes. Then the probes were blasted away, zooming off into space in four directions from the Moffship— to the north, south, east, and west—where they would travel to the farthest reaches of the galaxy in honor of their Imperial leader.

* * *

Trioculus was not the only three-eyed mutant who had a strong influence on the Empire. Perhaps even more important than Trioculus, and certainly more strange, was Triclops. Until recently Triclops had been an inmate in a ward for insane prisoners at the Imperial Reprogramming Institute on the planet Duro. Luke Skywalker rescued him on Duro, and then, for security reasons, sent Triclops to the fourth moon of Yavin to the headquarters of the Senate Planetary Intelligence Network, known as SPIN. There he was kept under observation and armed guard.

Soon after, the secret was out: Triclops, not Trioculus, was the long-lost son of the dead, evil Emperor Palpatine. That gave Triclops a legal claim to be the heir to the Imperial throne, the new ruler of the Empire. And that made him extremely dangerous, despite his previous claims to believe in peace, disarmament, and an end to all war.

Triclops slept much of the time, as if he were the victim of some unexplained sleeping sickness or powerful spell from the Dark Side. At the moment, the task of monitoring and observing Triclops fell upon Princess Leia. For the past few days she had also been busy studying the secret Jedi files Luke had brought back from his last trip to the Lost City of the Jedi. In her spare moments, Leia also worked on organizing her wedding to Han Solo, which was shaping up to be a much bigger event than they had planned.

Seated at a viewing screen in the SPIN conference room, Leia continued to monitor Triclops. She turned to glance at her brother, Luke Skywalker, who had just dropped by to discuss the matter.

"We've allowed Triclops to move freely about the first-level basement of the Senate building," Leia said, pointing to the screen. "He's sleepwalking again—it's as if he's in a trance. Look, Luke—he's gone to the storage area, and he's snooping around the old defense files."

"It's looking more and more like he is an Imperial spy after all," Luke said with a frown. "I'm afraid all of his sincere-sounding statements about hating the Empire may be nothing more than an act."

From the moment Luke and the others had met him, Triclops claimed to be an enemy of the Empire that his father, Emperor Palpatine, had commanded. Triclops opposed the now-deceased Darth Vader and all Imperial forces. According to Triclops, his opposition to the Empire was the reason he had been shut away inside Imperial insane asylums for his entire life. The Empire would not tolerate anyone who favored peace and disarmament, or who questioned its objectives, and Triclops was considered a great threat.

But Luke always questioned whether Triclops was telling the truth. The Rebel Alliance had discovered that Triclops had been kept alive by the Empire for one reason and one reason only: because he was a mad genius who often spoke aloud in his sleep, developing formulas and designs for new weapons systems.

"Yesterday we ran a medical examination on Triclops," Leia explained. "He appears to have in his mouth an Imperial implant of some sort in his right upper molar. This is no ordinary dental filling. It goes directly through the root of the tooth, into his brain. In fact, the implant seems to pick up the electromagnetic signals of his brain. Apparently it can broadcast Triclops's thoughts to the Imperial probe droids that have been invading our airspace."

"Is this a two-way system?" Luke asked. "Can the implant be used by the Empire to send electromagnetic signals into Triclops's brain?"

"That's a good question," Leia commented. "The answer seems to be yes, but only while he's in a state of very sound sleep."

Luke and Leia continued to watch the screen in the SPIN conference room, as Triclops disconnected an alarm and broke into a file storage bin.

"He certainly wants *something* desperately," Princess Leia said. "Do you think we should call in the sentries now?"

"Wait a moment," Luke cautioned.

They continued to watch calmly, knowing that Triclops's search of those particular files would gain him nothing of value. But as they exchanged worried glances, each was thinking the same thing: having Triclops in their midst might prove to be dangerous.

EEEE-AAAA-EEEE-AAAA . . . !

An airspace-intruder warning sounded. A second viewing screen turned on automatically, this one showing an Imperial probe droid descending over the rain forest. This particular probe droid was a huge floating black device with outstretched limbs that resembled spindly tentacles, just like the one the Al-

liance had once fought against on the ice-world of Hoth. Suddenly an Alliance X-wing flew to counter-attack.

"That's the third probe droid in two weeks that's entered the atmosphere of Yavin Four to spy on the senate," Leia said.

"They're very effective at deceiving our space shield radar defense system," Luke replied. "What we need is something that can locate Imperial probe droids long before they penetrate the atmosphere—a device to go after them and explode the probes before they even get this close to us."

"You mean something like an Omniprobe?" Leia asked.

"Exactly."

Leia rose from her chair excitedly. "Luke, that gives me an idea. I've been going through the data you brought back from the Lost City of the Jedi. I've searched the file menu you gave me, and there are lots of secret reports that you never accessed. That computer may still contain thousands of secrets that could prove crucial to our fight against the Empire. One of the files I discovered, that you didn't bring back, has a design for a new type of Omniprobe."

Ken, who was on vacation from school at Dagobah Tech, walked in just in time to hear what Leia had said. Ken was a Jedi Prince, and the newest member of the Alliance. "Hi, Luke,—hi, Leia," he said cheerfully. "I couldn't help overhearing you talking about my old school project. I'd almost forgotten about it."

"What school project?" Luke queried.

"The new Omniprobe. When I lived in the Lost City, Dee-Jay, my droid teacher, assigned me to study the blueprints for all the Omniprobes ever designed— both Alliance and Imperial—and he told me to try to invent a new Omniprobe, one that would utilize the best features of all of them. Well, I didn't know much about weaponry or laser systems, but Dee-Jay helped me, step by step, in coming up with a new Omniprobe design. That Omniprobe, if it were ever built, would be the perfect defense against Imperial probe droids."

"Do you think you remember enough about the design to redraw it?" Luke asked, raising his eyebrows in anticipation.

"Not likely," Ken replied. "I could make a rough sketch perhaps. But Dee-Jay did most of the work, and there were things about it I never did understand. But if you want the designs, they're still in the Jedi Library. I'm sure Dee-Jay could help us locate the file that has it."

"It sounds to me as if you and Ken should take another journey back to the Lost City," Leia said.

Suddenly they were distracted by the image on the viewing screen. Triclops was trembling, reacting to a pain in his head. Luke and Leia watched the screen as Triclops reached up to press his scarred temples. Then Triclops pushed two of his fingers into the back of his mouth, pressing on his upper molar.

Just then Triclops dropped to the floor and stopped moving. Luke and Leia exchanged a concerned glance. For a moment, they wondered whether Triclops was dead, or if he was just unconscious.

CHAPTER 2
Return to the Lost City

Far away on the planet Tatooine, a huge, sluglike old Hutt crawled slowly like a giant worm across the baking sands. His big, yellow, reptilian eyes scanned the horizon, but so far he had seen nothing but sandstorms and mirages.

Zorba the Hutt, whose braided white hair and beard were now covered with sand, had been squirming through the desert for several days, surviving without food or water, as Hutts have been known to do. "The grand moffs thought they'd get rid of me by tossing me into the Great Pit of Carkoon," he said to himself aloud, "but *no one* can outsmart a Hutt! And no one can digest a Hutt, either! I'll bet the Sarlacc's been nauseous for three days since he spit me out— a-haw-haw-haw . . . !"

Just then Zorba spied what he had been waiting to see. Off on the horizon, a metallic, boxlike shape was slowly rising from behind a distant sand dune. The object grew taller, until at last Zorba could see it rolling along on treads.

A sandcrawler!

"Surely my friends, the jawas, will give me a ride to the Mos Eisley spaceport!" Zorba said to himself.

Though Zorba called the jawas his "friends," the fast-talking desert traders known as the jawas despised all Hutts—especially Zorba. But Zorba was prepared to offer them a deal they couldn't refuse—a hundred slightly used Spin-and-Win machines from the Holiday Towers Hotel and Casino that Zorba owned back in Cloud City on the planet Bespin. Perhaps the machines could be resold by the jawas or installed in their sandcrawlers for entertainment.

"Once I get to Mos Eisley," Zorba continued, "I'll find a fearless cargo pilot willing to take me deep into the Null Zone, all the way to Space Station Scardia to see Kadann and his Prophets of the Dark Side. Just wait until the grand moffs see what I have in store for them. A-haw-haw-haw-haw-hawwwww . . . !"

Ken, the only human ever to have lived with the caretaker droids of the Lost City, was sure that he and Luke were getting closer to their destination. Ken had only departed from the Lost City on three occasions in his life: first when he tried to run away from home, then when he left in search of his lost computer notebook, and a third time after he had taken Luke Skywalker, Han Solo, and Chewbacca to the Lost City. On that last journey, Ken and Luke had taken special care to recall all the features of the twisting, weaving route through the heart of the rain forest—a path that eventually led to a hidden green round marble wall with a tubular transport in its center. However, the foliage of the forest had grown thicker since they had last been there together, and it was difficult to be certain they were going the right way.

Ken's pulse quickened as he thought about riding in the tubular transport, designed to travel down through miles of Yavin Four moonrock to reach the Lost City of the Jedi. The ancient Jedi Knights had constructed their secret hideaway in a buried cavern. That hideaway, the Alliance discovered, was the repository of Jedi files about the history of the galaxy and all its worlds.

Many explorers had searched for that tubular transport, but none of them had ever found it on their own. And Ken doubted that any ever would, because the rain forest in that region of Yavin Four was too dense, in spite of Trioculus's failed attempt once to burn it all down.

With every step he and Luke took, Ken thought about how exciting it would be to return to the Lost City, reunited with his feathery, four-eared pet mooka he had left behind.

At long last, Ken pushed away the leaves of a large bush. Beyond it Luke and Ken could finally see the green wall.

They entered the tubular transport, the metallic, bubblelike elevator with windows and streamlined controls. Then they took their positions alongside one another, getting ready for their descent.

"I can't wait to see the droids of the Lost City again, especially my teacher, Dee-Jay," Ken said. "He'll probably be astonished at all the wisdom I've gained since I left the Lost City and joined the Alliance."

"Wisdom?" Luke said. "Since when does a kid

who's twelve-going-on-thirteen have true wisdom?"

"I've learned a lot from my experiences, Luke," Ken shot back, as he pulled the lever in the tubular transport, causing it to drop with the speed of a spaceship blasting off.

WHIIIIIIISH!

"How many kids my age do you know who have seen Banthas, jawas, Tusken Raiders, and bounty hunters?" Ken continued, when he had caught his breath. He gripped the handrails very tightly. "And how many twelve-year-olds do you know who have been to Cloud City, met up with Zorba the Hutt *and* Trioculus, and zoomed all the way to Hologram Fun World—"

"Unfortunately, Ken, attaining true wisdom has little to do with any of that," Luke said, looking at the faintly glowing moonrock that zipped past them as they rapidly descended. "Wisdom has to do with how much insight you have about life, and your level of maturity. And it seems to me you could do with a little advancement on that score."

Ken felt a strange sensation in his stomach as they plunged toward the vast cavern. "This is better than the rides at Hologram Fun World."

Finally, the tubular transport reached the bottom of the seemingly endless elevator shaft. Then the door slid open and they stepped out.

Off in the distance, there were dozens of droids going about their maintenance work, keeping the city functioning mechanically, without any human beings.

Luke and Ken descended a flight of stairs and

then walked along Jedi Lane. They could see the power cubes, computer chambers, and mechanized towers, as well as the many dome-houses that served as dwellings for the Jedi caretaker droids.

"I can hardly believe I'm really back here," Ken said, breathing rapidly with anticipation. He glanced around as fast as his head could twist, looking in all directions.

"Someday, maybe we'll find out how you got here in the first place," Luke said.

"I told you how I got here, Luke," Ken replied, as they continued walking up Jedi Lane. "When I was little, a Jedi Knight in a brown robe brought me here—after my parents died, I think. I only wish I knew who my parents were."

"And who was that Jedi Knight in the brown robe?" Luke asked.

"Obi-Wan Kenobi always wore a brown robe, didn't he?" Ken inquired.

"Yes, but he wasn't the only one who did."

"But there were only a few Jedi Knights still alive when I was born," Ken replied. "It *could* have been him, couldn't it?"

"I don't know," Luke said. "Obi-Wan never told me about it. He never even hinted."

Ken touched the crystal he wore around his neck, a half sphere attached to a thin, silver chain. The droids of the Lost City had told Ken he had been wearing that birthstone when he was brought to them as a young child. As much as he wanted to remember those days, his memories of that time were very foggy.

Suddenly Ken heard familiar-sounding footsteps coming from behind them. "HC!" Ken exclaimed, turning to confirm his guess.

HC-100 was a Homework Correction Droid who looked like See-Threepio, but with a round mouth and a circular belly. The fact that even HC was now a welcome sight to Ken's eyes was a sure sign of how much Ken had missed the Lost City, his childhood home.

"Well, Ken, at last you've returned to continue your lessons," HC stated. He swiveled his head to stare at Luke. "Oh, hello, Commander Skywalker. So good to see that you've brought Ken back to us."

"I'm afraid Ken hasn't returned here to continue his studies," Luke explained. "Ken's one of the brightest students at a very special school, Dagobah Tech. At the moment he's on vacation. Ken's classmates are the sons and daughters of the scientists who work at DRAPAC, our fortress, on Mount Yoda on the planet Dagobah."

HC-100 twisted his body at the waist as he bent to peer at Ken. "Well then, perhaps you can think up a way to plug the hole in the ground beneath our decoy tubular transport."

"What decoy tubular transport?" Ken asked. "What hole in the ground?"

"A botanist searching for rare plants happened to come upon the new green marble wall last week, quite by chance," HC continued without hesitation. "He entered the decoy tubular transport, not knowing what it was, and it plunged downward, almost sending him to a fiery death!"

"But I still don't understand, HC," Ken interrupted. "What do you mean by a decoy tubular transport? And why did the botanist almost die?"

"I can explain," said a deep-sounding voice.

Ken turned. Walking up the path toward them was DJ-88, or "Dee-Jay" as Ken called him. The tall, wise-looking old droid's ruby eyes were shining brightly at Ken and Luke. Ken suddenly felt a flood of memories as he recalled his many happy experiences with Dee-Jay, the powerful caretaker droid and teacher who had raised him.

"Dee-Jay, it's great to see you!" Ken shouted. "And Zeebo! Come here, little fellow. . . ."

Zeebo, Ken's four-eared pet mooka, leaped from Dee-Jay's arms and went running up to Ken, jumping all over him. Ken scratched behind each of Zeebo's four ears. "Hey there, Zeebo, how've you been?"

"Kssssssshhhhh," Zeebo said in a purr of contentment. "Kssssssshhhhhh!"

"Greetings, Commander Skywalker, and welcome," Dee-Jay said. "This is indeed a splendid honor. I'm grateful you've brought Ken back to visit his home. You look a bit taller, Ken, than when I last saw you. And perhaps you're a bit more experienced now in the ways of the world."

"Quite a bit more experienced, thanks," Ken assured him. "It's really good to be back, Dee-Jay."

"Pleased to hear that you still respect your old droid teacher," Dee-Jay said. He then invited them all to walk with him over to the Jedi Library.

"As HC was saying," Dee-Jay explained, "to defend ourselves against the Imperials, a long time ago we droids of the Lost City went Topworld into the jungle and built a second circular marble wall. This entrance was a decoy to mislead spies and those who wished to locate and destroy us or steal the Jedi's secrets from our library files. Whoever boards the decoy tubular transport is taken down to a dark damp cave. Although they would be able to make their way out, their search for the Lost City would reach a dead end. But that all changed when the tremors struck recently."

"What did the tremors do, Dee-Jay?" Ken asked.

"They caused a big crack in the ground," Dee-Jay explained. "No longer does the decoy transport descend to the cave. Now it opens up on a big hole that drops to a fiery river of molten lava."

As they arrived at the Jedi Library, Dee-Jay added, "Here in this building, we're researching how to repair the hole, so no innocent travelers in the jungle will be in mortal danger if they happen to stumble upon the decoy. But it's a difficult problem to solve, because the ground there is now so very unstable."

Luke, Ken, and the two droids entered and walked past row after row of shelves containing old documents and historical records from many planets. One by one, Dee-Jay had been inputting the data from those records into the Jedi master computer, just as he had been programmed to do back in the days when there had been many Jedi Knights. If by some improbable chance the Jedi Knights were ever to flourish again, those records would be invaluable. In the meantime, as it was needed, selected files of information would be released to the Rebel Alliance through Ken and Luke Skywalker.

"I see that the master computer is on-line," Ken said, noticing the computer's main menu of files and operations that filled its screen. "Commander Skywalker and I need the blueprint you helped me design for the Omniprobe device. Remember my homework assignment?"

"Of course," Dee-Jay replied. "Seems to me I was the one who did almost all of the technical work."

"Let's see if I can still locate the master file," Ken said. He sat at the controls and tried to program the computer to bring up the data he wanted. But he punched the wrong code by mistake and instead brought up a file called *Imperial Space Stations*.

"You won't find the Omniprobe blueprint there," Dee-Jay said. "But you might discover in that file secrets of Space Station Scardia and other major Imperial outposts located in deep space."

"Scardia!" Ken exclaimed. "That's the home of Kadann and the Imperial Prophets of the Dark Side!"

"Correct," Dee-Jay replied. "And speaking of Kadann, very recently he made some very troublesome new prophecies. We've only just learned of them. For instance—"

Dee-Jay leaned over Ken's shoulder and touched the computer controls with his metallic fingers. Instantly, the screen was filled with four-line prophecies made by the black-bearded dwarf Kadann, Supreme Prophet of the Dark Side. Dee-Jay enlarged one particular prophecy until it filled the screen:

When the Jedi Knight
Becomes a captive of Scardia,
Then shall the Jedi Prince
Betray the Lost City.

"That prophecy talks about a Jedi Knight being a captive of Scardia," Ken said. Turning to Luke, he continued, "I guess that means you, Luke, or perhaps Leia being a captive of Space Station Scardia and the Prophets of the Dark Side. It also talks about a Jedi Prince—that must be me!—betraying the Lost City to the Empire. But that could *never* happen!"

"I certainly hope not," Dee-Jay said. "This city is a sacred place, and no Imperial must ever set foot in it."

"No Imperial ever shall," Ken replied with confidence.

"Kadann has no special powers to see the future," Luke said. "Remember what Yoda told me: *'Always in motion is the future.'* That means that the future isn't something that's fixed ahead of time, waiting to happen."

"So the future is always changing, always evolving up until the moment it actually arrives?" Ken asked.

"Exactly," Luke explained. "And that's why we all decide our own destinies by the choices we make."

Ken nodded. He had made a choice—the choice to join the Rebel Alliance. And that choice had influenced his destiny. But there was one choice he would certainly never make. No matter what Kadann predicted, Ken would *never* betray the Lost City!

CHAPTER 3
A Time for Feasting

Zorba the Hutt had arrived at the home of the Prophets of the Dark Side. After negotiating a ride from the jawas, a cargo spaceship pilot had flown Zorba all the way from Mos Eisley on Tatooine into the dreaded Null Zone of deep space.

When the Prophets of the Dark Side learned that Zorba had come with valuable information, they honored the Hutt with a huge banquet in Scardia's formal dining hall. The refined prophets, who had elegant manners, and who always dined using the finest black linen and spotless black plates, winced at seeing Zorba's slovenly ways. Zorba gobbled everything in sight and burped repeatedly, rudely displaying his thick, slobbering, drooling tongue.

High Prophet Jedgar, seated at Zorba's right at the long banquet table, gasped in shock as Zorba splattered his serving of zoochberry dumplings, staining Jedgar's sparkling robe.

"Ahhhhhh," Zorba moaned with pleasure, reaching for another stewed Mynock bat. "Delicious. And I must compliment you prophets on your fried Bantha steaks."

Zorba glanced around the room as he rudely

chomped on a piece of raw rancor-beast liver, which hung out of the side of his mouth and dripped rancor-blood down his braided white beard.

"You give the impression you haven't had a bite to eat for an eternity," Kadann said.

"Hardly a bite for days," Zorba replied. "After the Mouth of Sarlacc spit me out—Hutts are not digestible, you know—I crawled for ten long, hot days through the Tatooine desert, surviving by eating cactabushes, thorns and all. Finally I saw a sandcrawler. To get a ride to the Mos Eisley Spaceport, I promised the jawas a hundred barely used, practically new Spin-and-Win machines from the Holiday Towers Hotel and Casino. Then I had to promise to pay fifty gemstones to get a cargo pilot to

bring me here. But I made the sacrifice because of my patriotic duty to the Empire. I have come to tell you that the Imperial grand moffs are traitors. They've been plotting to destroy you!"

"I've already alerted several star destroyers to be on the lookout for the Moffship, to arrest the grand moff leaders and bring them here to stand trial," Kadann said.

Zorba stuffed his mouth with two more zoochberry dumplings, chewing them up and gulping them down before Kadann finished his sentence. Then Zorba's wandering eyes fell on the stylish glass cases that decorated the banquet room, cases filled with ancient collectibles that Kadann had stolen from throughout the galaxy.

"You certainly have enchanting relics, Kadann," Zorba said, chewing loudly. "Which leads me to ask whether you've managed to plunder any relics from the Lost City of the Jedi."

Kadann narrowed his gaze and stared intensely at the blubbery Hutt. "What do you know of the Lost City?" Kadann asked.

"Only that Trioculus tried to locate the Lost City because he wanted to capture the Jedi Prince named Ken who used to live there," Zorba replied. "But Trioculus failed."

"Yes, and he paid a large price for his failure," Kadann said gruffly. "I told Trioculus to find the Lost City of the Jedi and destroy the Jedi Prince, or his reign over the Empire would be brief. I knew he would never succeed, but we have no choice, we must all live out our destinies. That prophecy came true, as all of mine do."

"*URRRRRP!* Of course. Congratulations on the accuracy of your prophecies, Kadann," Zorba said. And then he burped again. "*URRRRRRRRP!* By the way, it's been said that your prophets go to great lengths and quite a lot of effort to make certain that your prophecies come true. There isn't any truth to that rumor, is there?"

"Where have you heard that?" Kadann asked with a scowl.

"I've heard it said by the grand moffs. They claim that anyone who has as many spies, assassins, bounty hunters, and bribe-payers as you do could make the future turn out any way he likes."

"That's an outrageous lie!" High Prophet Jedgar interrupted angrily.

"My sentiments exactly," Zorba said. "I thought it was a lie when I heard the traitors say it."

"Although Trioculus failed in his quest to locate the Lost City, Supreme Prophet Kadann shall find it soon enough," High Prophet Jedgar declared with assurance.

"And when you do, Kadann, I'll bet you'll add quite a few relics to your splendid collection," Zorba said. "A-haw-haw-haw . . ."

"I'm not looking for the Lost City to collect Jedi relics," Kadann said with a little smile. "I'm far more interested in the master computer that's said to be inside the Jedi Library."

"Yes," High Prophet Jedgar agreed. "It contains all the secrets of the Jedi Knights. That information could be used to destroy the Rebel Alliance forever."

In a very clumsy move, Zorba accidentally spilled some juice on the handmade carpet from Endor. Then he rolled his sluglike tail over the stains, pressing down with the weight of several tons. Kadann nearly choked as Zorba ruined his favorite carpet that had taken a hundred Ewoks five years to make.

"Of all the explorers who have searched for the Lost City," Zorba continued, "I don't know of any who has lived to tell the tale."

"*I* shall live to tell the tale," Kadann said, wiping his lips as he munched his Bantha steak. "The Jedi Prince, Ken, will lead me there personally."

Kadann broke into a very broad smile, which

prompted the other prophets to smile too. Then they all began to snicker and laugh. However, Zorba's laugh was the loudest of them all. "A-haw-haw-haw-haw-haw . . . !"

Luke Skywalker flew his airspeeder low above the trees of the rain forest on Yavin Four, with Ken holding on tightly behind him. As they made their way back to the Alliance Senate building, the airspeeder zigzagged around the pointy spires of the ancient temples and pyramids that rose above the canopy of thick green leaves.

In the lounge outside the Senate conference room, Princess Leia took a few moments away from her work for the Alliance, so that she could read the wedding guest list to Han. Ever since Zorba the Hutt had spoiled Han and Leia's plans to quickly elope at Hologram Fun World, the two of them had been planning a wedding at which hundreds of guests would fly in from halfway across the galaxy.

See-Threepio was assisting Leia with the guest list and banquet seating chart, while barrel-shaped Artoo-Detoo scooted around on his wheels.

"Han, do you think Admiral Ackbar should sit with the delegation from Calamari?" Leia asked. "Or should we put him at the table with the top Alliance officials like Mon Mothma?"

"Hmmh?" Han said. He was sitting on a floating cushion with a thick, secret SPIN report in his lap— a report about Triclops. "Sounds okay to me, I guess."

"*What* sounds okay, Han?" Leia asked with annoyance. "Which seating location do you prefer for Admiral Ackbar at the wedding reception?"

"Whichever you like, Leia," Han commented, not really paying any attention. "Makes no difference, as far as I can tell."

"Aren't you interested in helping to plan the most important day of our lives, Han?" Leia asked.

"Face it, Leia," Han said, "I'm just not cut out to plan big social events. The biggest party I ever had—my housewarming party for my sky house—was strictly informal. I did the cooking myself with Chewie, and I brought in a Corellian band to provide all the entertainment. That was the extent of it. But big weddings, that's a Bantha of a different color."

"You're not interested in anything new and different, Han," Leia said, "unless it's some daredevil feat—something so dangerous you can get yourself killed doing it."

"Well, a guy *could* get killed at a wedding," Han replied. "A guy could slip on the floor while dancing with his bride and end up breaking his neck."

"This conversation is getting *ridiculous*," Leia said in frustration. "Just tell me this, do you think that Chewbacca should sit at the Wookiee table or with us? I was thinking he should be the host of the Wookiee table, but since he's your Best Man, he should probably sit with us. What do you think?"

"Chewie should sit with us," said Luke Skywalker, joining the conversation as he entered the lounge with Ken. "From what I can tell, he's not too fond of some of his Wookiee relatives."

"How did things go with your mission, Luke?" Leia asked. She smiled, glad to see that he and Ken had returned safely. "Did you find the plans for the Omniprobe?"

"We sure did."

Luke unfolded the Omniprobe blueprints that he and Ken had brought back from the Lost City of the Jedi, and showed the plans to Leia. "The next step," Luke said, "is to get our engineering research team to build a prototype model."

Ken glanced over at Han, who seemed very comfortable lying back on his floating pillow, studying the report. "What are you reading that's so engrossing, Han?" Ken asked.

"The latest SPIN report on Triclops," Han replied. "Seems that before they could attempt surgery to remove the implant in his right upper molar, the SPIN examiners found out that Triclops's tooth has a very deep nerve root that goes all the way to his brain. They thought they could easily extract it, but it turns out it's a very unusual condition. Pulling that particular tooth could prove to be very dangerous. Right now we're on hold for the operation."

* * *

In the meantime, the Alliance did nothing to prevent Triclops from being able to sneak into the file storage area again. Luke deliberately planted a file on the Lost City of the Jedi that was filled with disinformation—misleading facts, a phony map, and false coordinates that would lead the Imperials away from the actual Lost City, and toward the decoy green wall the droids had built. If the Imperials took the bait and went to the decoy wall, they would end up in the dark cave—perhaps falling into the underground river of molten lava!

That night, Triclops began sleepwalking again. He went to the file storage area, where he located the file on the Lost City and memorized its contents. Triclops then replaced it, trying to make it look as though nothing in the file storage area had been disturbed.

While this was going on, the Alliance deliberately relaxed its air defense network. An Imperial probe droid approached the Alliance Senate again, and this time it was deliberately permitted to come close enough to pick up Triclops's broadcasted message. The message was from his thought waves, as his thoughts were broadcast by the tiny Imperial implant in his molar tooth.

Afterward, a few X-wing starfighters were sent up to chase the Imperial probe droid away. The X-wings's instructions were to let the probe escape and deliberately avoid shooting it down, so the disinformation from Triclops would reach the Prophets of the Dark Side.

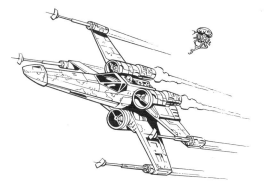

CHAPTER 4
The Trial of the Grand Moffs

At Space Station Scardia, a trial was about to begin. Four grand moffs had been arrested in their Moffship by the crew of an Imperial starfighter. Grand Moff Hissa, chained to his hover-chair, and Grand Moffs Thistleborn, Dunhausen, and Muzzer, with their hands chained behind their backs, stood accused of treason against the Empire.

Kadann entered the Chamber of Dark Justice, preparing to sit in judgment. The dwarf took his position on an ornate chair that had once belonged to an ancient king of Duro. To make Kadann appear taller than he actually was, the chair was placed on a raised stage.

Defeen, the wolflike alien who had recently been promoted by the Prophets of the Dark Side to the position of interrogator supreme, prowled in front of a jury of five prophets.

"The trial of the grand moffs now beginsssss!" Defeen hissed. "I call the first witnesssssss—Zorba the Hutt!"

"But Zorba the Hutt is dead!" Grand Moff Hissa exclaimed, gasping.

Zorba, very much alive, wiggled through the

round doorway and squirmed to the witness stand.
"Thought you'd seen me for the last time? Wrong!"
Zorba said tauntingly, glaring at the four accused
men with his big, yellow reptilian eyes. "A-haw-haw-
haw . . . !"

Kadann began the proceedings by picking up a
blue chalklike ball from a collection of colored balls at
his side. He crushed it in his right hand. As if by some
supernatural power, a chilling wind suddenly swept
across the Chamber of Dark Justice, blowing the blue
chalk onto the uniforms of the four grand moffs.

But there was nothing supernatural about the
wind. At the push of a hidden button, Kadann could
make a cold breeze blow from any direction inside
the chamber. And at the push of another button, he
could make the walls resonate with an echo, giving
his voice the sound of greater authority.

"Blue is the color of shame and disgrace," Grand Moff Hissa whispered to Grand Moff Muzzer, who stood alongside him. "This trial will be a total sham, a show and nothing more. It's obvious Kadann has already made up his mind that we're guilty."

"Grand moffssssss," Defeen said with a scowl, pointing a furry, clawed hand at the defendants. "You are charged with breaking your pledgessss of loyalty to Kadann, who is now the ruler of the Empire." Defeen then trained his beady red eyes at Zorba, who was grinning from one side of his huge head to the other. "I have here a sworn statement from Zorba the Hutt stating that you tried to restore to the Imperial throne the disgraced leader, Trioculussssss."

The charges were given, and then the trial began.

In his bedroom in his tower house on Yavin Four, Luke Skywalker could faintly hear the sound of someone turning pages and muttering facts from a science textbook. Ken must be already wide awake, he concluded. Luke had moved an extra floating bed over by the door so that Ken, who was due to go back to school at Dagobah Tech after the wedding of Han and Leia, would have a place to sleep.

Luke opened his eyes and saw Ken sitting up on his floating bed, trying to memorize a list of atomic weights. Then Luke heard the footsteps of someone bounding up the circular stairwell that led to the room at the top of the tower.

A moment later, Princess Leia opened the door a crack and peeked into the room. "Luke, are you awake?" And then she smiled at the Jedi Prince. "Oh, good morning, Ken."

"Hi, Leia," Ken said, then he buried his nose in his atomic element chart.

Leia handed her brother Luke a medical research report. "Luke, SPIN medical specialists have determined how to deal with the mind control implant in Triclops's tooth, and put an end to Kadann's long-distance penetration of Triclops's mind. Our medical staff says that if they had some *macaab* mushrooms, they could produce a chemical that could deactivate the implant permanently."

Luke tied his robe and slid his feet into the slippers at the side of his floating bed. "If Triclops isn't actually a spy of his own free will," Luke said, "by destroying the implant, we would then give Triclops a chance to prove he really does oppose the Empire."

"There's one problem," Leia explained. "Macaab mushrooms are extremely rare. The nearest planet where they grow is Arzid."

Ken remembered studying about Arzid—a hot, dense world with macaab mushroom forests everywhere, and large spiderlike creatures called arachnors. Ken closed up his textbook and put away his element chart, thinking to himself how much he had always wanted to see an arachnor.

"Let's go to Arzid, Luke," Ken said. "We could still be back in time for the wedding, couldn't we?"

Luke wasted no time coming to a decision. It was worth the effort to find out if Triclops could be freed of Imperial mind control. After discussing the matter further with Leia and Ken, Luke announced that he would depart with Ken, Artoo-Detoo, See-Threepio, and Chewbacca in a modified Rendili Star Drive Y-wing. Unlike the standard Y-wing spaceship, which was only big enough for a two-man crew and one astromech droid like Artoo, the modified Rendili Y-wing was large enough for a crew of four.

Princess Leia and Han Solo would stay behind, so they could continue monitoring Triclops. That would also give Leia an opportunity to send out the last few invitations to their wedding, while Han set up the THX Super-Sound System for the dance that would follow the wedding ceremony. It was a perfect plan—if all went according to schedule.

At Space Station Scardia, the trial of the grand moffs was finally drawing to a conclusion. Kadann's booming voice echoed powerfully. "Grand moffs, you will now plead guilty to disloyalty and treason," he said. "After I accept your guilty pleas, I will listen to your requests for mercy."

"Each in turn now," said Defeen, baring his wolflike fangs. "Make your guilty pleasssss or you will be charged with insssssurection and unlawful ressssssistance!"

"Guilty," Grand Moff Thistleborn confessed reluctantly.

"Guilty," Grand Moff Dunhausen agreed.

"Guilty," Grand Moff Muzzer concurred.

"Not guilty," Grand Moff Hissa said. A shocked silence fell upon the Chamber of Dark Justice. "I deserve the respect due to an Imperial war hero," he continued. "I lost my arms and legs in service to you, Kadann, on a mission to Duro, trying to recapture Triclops when he escaped. And I demand that you arrest this lying Hutt who would obviously say anything he thought you wanted to hear!"

"Sssssilence!" Defeen hissed. "Grand Moff Hissa, we have a file on you that's thissssss thick," Defeen said, holding his clawed hands apart to show the exact thickness. "We have lotssss of evidence against you!"

Kadann turned to the five jurors. "Three grand moffs have pleaded guilty, but Grand Moff Hissa says that he is innocent. I have just written my prophecy of what your verdict on Hissa will be, and I hereby provide it to you. Study it carefully. But do not let my prophecy influence you in any way, because that would be unfair."

"A-haw-haw-haw . . ." Zorba the Hutt laughed.

The jurors opened the sealed envelope and studied Kadann's prophecy. They whispered among themselves for almost a full minute. Then Kadann asked them, "Have you reached a verdict?"

High Prophet Jedgar, as foreman of the jury, stood to his full towering height. He thrust out his chest beneath his glittering black robe, and spoke. "We find Grand Moff Hissa guilty. The grand moffs are all guilty, but we conclude that Hissa is the guiltiest."

"Thank you," Kadann said. "You shall now hear your sentences for treachery! Grand Moff Thistleborn,

three years of hard labor in the rock quarries of the scorching planet, Bnach. No prisoner has ever survived the rock quarries for more than a year. Perhaps you will be the first to do so."

Kadann turned his gaze to the next convicted man. "Grand Moff Dunhausen, you're to be sent to the Imperial Correctional Center on the frozen world of Hoth for four years. All prisoners there freeze to death within three years. But you seem like hardy stock. I expect you'll set a new survival record, and when you return, you'll have a better attitude about your duties to the Empire and the Prophets of the Dark Side."

Kadann's gaze moved on down the line of defendants. "Grand Moff Muzzer, you shall serve for five years as the lowly sentry at a small Imperial outpost on the planet Arzid, the planet of macaab mushrooms, tentacle-bushes, and deadly arachnors. Perhaps you shall meet with better fortune than the last sentry, who stumbled into an arachnor web his first month on Arzid and was eaten by those hungry giant spiders."

Kadann now stared at Grand Moff Hissa, who in protest was shaking his head, rattling the chain that fastened his prisoner's collar to his hover-chair. "Grand Moff Hissa, because Zorba the Hutt assures me that your crimes are more serious than those of your companions, and because you led the plot to return Trioculus to his position of power, I sentence you to die a cruel and unusual death. You shall be starved, and when you are mad and insane with hunger, you shall be served your last meal. It shall be a meal of biscuits that have live parasites baked into them. The parasites will begin eating you from inside the pit of your stomach and will work their way slowly to your outermost layer of flesh."

"A-haw-haw-haw-haw-hawwwww . . . !" Zorba roared, his blubbery body vibrating so much that it shook the entire room like a tremor.

Suddenly Prophet Gornash entered the chamber and whispered to Kadann. "My dear Supreme Prophet Kadann," Gornash began, "it seems that a probe droid has just returned from Yavin Four with information from Triclops. Triclops has just provided us with the precise location of the entrance to the Lost City of the Jedi!"

Kadann smiled. His spy, Triclops, had done well. And all the more impressive given the fact that Triclops didn't even *know* that he was an Imperial spy!

CHAPTER 5
Web of Disaster

Luke Skywalker disengaged the hyperdrive thrusters of their modified Y-wing spaceship. Then he and Chewbacca navigated skillfully past the gigantic green fire storms that shot up from the surface of the sun known as Tiki-hava. Those fire storms spread an eerie glow for thousands of miles. When Luke's spaceship finally soared past the space-glow, they could see the gray planet Arzid directly in front of them.

The spaceship glided to a soft landing in a valley surrounded by giant mushroom forests. Ken was the

first to hurry down the entrance ramp to the soft, spongy ground of the planet.

"*Zneeeech Kboooop!*" Artoo-Detoo tooted.

"Artoo is right—I suggest you pay attention to where you're walking, Master Ken," See-Threepio exclaimed. "Watch out for arachnor webs—they're horribly sticky and rather huge. And keep your eyes to the ground, and beware of tentacle-bushes."

"What's a tentacle-bush?" Ken asked.

"Just like the name suggests," Threepio explained. "A small plant with long, thin tentacles that reach out to snatch little rodents."

Luke Skywalker hoisted a portable stun-cannon to his shoulder. "This may prove to be useful if we meet up with any arachnors."

Ken glanced around at the nearby mushroom forest. "Cool!" he exclaimed. "There's macaab mushrooms everywhere up on that hill. Let's go, last one there is a Kowakian monkey-lizard!"

"Wait up, Master Ken!" See-Threepio shouted. But Ken was already far ahead of everyone.

It was also the first time Luke had been in a macaab mushroom forest. He too was quite overwhelmed to see the range of sizes, from the small mushrooms that hugged the ground like little flowers, to the tree-size macaabs that towered high above them.

HISSSSSSSS!

Ken's heart skipped a beat. He glanced over his shoulder and saw a spidery arachnor twice his size crawling down a huge mushroom.

Luke saw it too, and he began firing his portable stun-cannon as he walked toward the spider. But he didn't notice the thin green tentacle that was slithering along the ground near his right boot. Suddenly the tentacle twisted around Luke's ankle and gave a sharp tug, pulling him to the ground headfirst as his legs slid out from under him. The stun-cannon fell from Luke's hands and slid partway down a steep embankment.

"Groooowwwf!" Chewbacca growled, heading down the embankment to recover the weapon.

But as soon as Chewbacca reached out for the stun-cannon, a spindly tentacle wrapped around his left ankle. The tentacle-bush tightened and squeezed, toppling the big Wookiee right into some thorny shrubs.

"Rooooarrrf!" Chewbacca moaned in protest.

"Well, don't blame *me*!" Threepio scolded, as he took a few cautious steps down the embankment. "I *warned* you about those tentacle-bushes—obviously no one was listening."

"Just a second, Chewie," Ken shouted. "I'll get the stun-cannon!"

"Wait, Ken!" Luke yelled.

But Ken didn't wait. He bounded down the slippery embankment. And as he reached for the stun-cannon, he just kept sliding, down and down until he found himself far past the point where Chewbacca had fallen. In fact, Ken slid so far, he brushed up against an arachnor web at the bottom of the hill. Ken stuck to the web like molasses.

"Hey, get me out of this!" Ken screamed. As he shouted, out of the corner of his eye, Ken could make out a strange tower just beyond the forest at the bottom of the hill.

Back near the top of the hill, Chewbacca, who was covered with prickly thorns, growled in outrage. "Rowwwooooof!" Chewbacca moaned, unable to loosen the tentacle from his ankle with his big hairy paws.

Luke had more success than Chewbacca. Drawing out his lightsaber, he aimed the green blade of the laser at the tentacle that was still gripping tightly onto his boot. With one swift swing of his blade, Luke sliced the tentacle in two. Then he jumped to his feet and hurried down the embankment to attempt to free Ken and Chewbacca.

"I'll be right back, Chewie," Luke said as he passed the big Wookiee and continued down the embankment. "I've got to get to Ken first. Those arachnor webs are like quicksand—the more he struggles, the harder it will be to get him out!"

Luke was right. As Ken wiggled his arms the sticky web seemed to wrap around him like a cocoon.

"Oh dear, oh my! I knew we never should have come here," See-Threepio complained, keeping his eye sensors trained on Luke, who was now nearly at the bottom of the embankment, alongside Ken.

Suddenly Artoo burst out with a warning. *"BDwooEEEEP TWeeEEEG!"*

"Watch out, Master Luke!" Threepio translated. "There's an arachnor climbing down the mushroom right behind you!"

Luke drew his lightsaber, and he made a sudden lunge toward the arachnor. Failing to destroy it in the first sweep of his glowing green blade, Luke suddenly felt his movement hindered by a sticky substance—the arachnor was weaving a web around him!

Luke aimed his lightsaber at the arachnor's long, spindly legs, slicing them one by one. But with every passing second, Luke felt his shoulders, then his legs, then both his arms trapped as if he were stuck in glue.

Luke dealt the arachnor a fatal blow, right at the gnawing mouth on the underbelly between its spidery legs. A split second later Luke's lightsaber slipped away from him as his hand became caught in the web. Luke couldn't reach down for it. All he could do was crane his neck upward, to check out a strange sound that was coming from the sky.

FWOOOOOOSH!

Standing at the edge of the embankment, See-Threepio saw what Luke heard. The droid glanced up and spotted a spacecraft appearing out of the clouds, descending toward a small tower that rose above the mushroom forest.

"Ftwiiiiing ChEEEpz!"

"You're right, Artoo," Threepio said. "That spaceship appears to be an Imperial command speeder. And that tower down there—why, I didn't notice it before—it may actually be a small Imperial sentry outpost!"

The Imperial command speeder landed near the small Imperial outpost. No sooner had the spaceship set down than five Imperial stormtroopers stepped outside, bringing with them the prisoner who was to serve as a sentry on this miserable planet: Grand Moff Muzzer. It didn't take long for them to detect the presence of other humans nearby, and at once, two of the stormtroopers set out to look for them.

Hiding behind a tall mushroom near the top of the embankment, See-Threepio and Artoo-Detoo watched. Still trying to free his ankle from the tentacle-bush, Chewbacca looked down the hill to see what was happening also.

"Woooooofff!" Chewbacca barked.

"*Tweeeez BdOOOOpz!*" Artoo beeped, anxiously rotating his entire body as his tiny radar reflector popped up from his dome.

"Artoo is quite right, Chewbacca," Threepio said in a soft voice. "Shshshshhhh—you've got to be quiet, or else those stormtroopers will discover us, too."

At the bottom of the embankment, the stormtroopers were boasting to one another about their discovery of two humans trapped in arachnor webs.

"Well, if it isn't Commander Skywalker. Quite a catch!" the leader of the stormtroopers said. "This should be worth a big promotion!"

Luke tried once again to reach his lightsaber, but he was so tangled in the sticky web, it was hopeless.

One of the stormtroopers removed a small stun-beam pistol from his utility belt. "This should keep you both under control until Kadann gets to talk to you," the stormtrooper said. He fired, targeting both of the Rebel Alliance prisoners.

The stun-beam had precisely the expected effect. Luke and Ken were rendered half unconscious, barely able to move or think at all, let alone concentrate on the Force.

Then the Imperials turned their pulse-mass generator on the arachnor webs, melting the webs completely. Without the support of the webs to hold them up, Luke and Ken both tumbled to the ground, scarcely able to bend their limbs because of the effects of the stun-beam.

Luke and Ken were quickly overpowered. Their hands were pulled behind their backs and fastened with Imperial locking wrist-cuffs. Then a stormtropper snatched Luke's lightsaber as a souvenir to present to Kadann, plucking it from the ground where Luke had dropped it. The Imperial turned the lightsaber on, gleefully watching its green, glowing blade.

The stormtroopers forced Luke and Ken to their feet, pushing them along. The prisoners' stunned legs could barely move, but they were forced to march all the way to the Imperial command speeder.

"Oh my, oh no!" Threepio said, still watching from a safe distance away. "We need a plan, a plan at once! This situation has gotten quite out of hand for the likes of two droids and a Wookiee!"

The Imperial command speeder blasted off, leaving the mushroom planet. The destination of the space-

ship was a huge golden craft beyond Tiki-hava: the *Scardia Voyager.*

Aboard the *Scardia Voyager,* Kadann sat in his upraised chair on the navigation deck. He peered out into the darkness of space, calmly observing the approach of the Imperial command speeder. High Prophet Jedgar and Prophet Gornash stood on either side of him.

No sooner did the command speeder dock aboard the *Scardia Voyager* than two new prisoners were brought before Kadann in chains. As the Supreme Prophet realized who the prisoners were, he smiled with a dark glee of vengeance.

"It would appear that your days of fighting for the Rebel Alliance have at last come to an end, Skywalker," Kadann proclaimed wickedly. He arose from his chair and approached the prisoners.

Luke pulled at the Imperial wrist-cuffs, trying to

use Jedi powers to unfasten them. But it was to no avail. He was still too stunned to concentrate and use the Force.

"Is there a problem, Skywalker?" Kadann inquired. "Surely you didn't think your foolhardy Rebel heroics would go on forever, did you? And you—" Kadann turned to Ken and noticed that he was shivering. "Is it too cold for you in the *Scardia Voyager*? Perhaps you'd care for a cup of hot tea."

Kadann poured a cup of tea from the steaming kettle on the stand beside him. Beside the kettle was a tray of biscuits. "Here, this should warm you up."

Though Luke was still groggy, he was awake enough to warn Ken not to drink the tea Kadann was offering him. "Don't do it," Luke cautioned. "It might contain avabush, and—"

But before Luke even finished his sentence, Ken swallowed several gulps of tea from the cup Kadann held up to his lips. Then he glanced at Commander Skywalker. "Sorry, Luke," Ken said. "I was freezing—I couldn't help it. I'm much warmer now."

"Commander Skywalker objects," Kadann said, "because he suspects that this is avabush tea, made from avabush spice, a truth serum of sorts. But surely you don't think that I would do such a thing as give a boy truth serum, do you? I think your friend Luke Skywalker is jealous of the freedom I can offer you, young man," Kadann continued. "He knows that his Jedi powers are no match for the powers of the Dark Side."

"Jedi powers are more than a match for any

powers *you* can claim, Kadann," Luke retorted.

Narrowing his gaze to a mere slit, Kadann spied the dome-shaped crystal birthstone that Ken wore around his neck on a silver chain. "Don't you think it's time we introduced ourselves?" Kadann said. "Tell me your name."

Ken was determined to give a false name. But just as he was trying to think one up, he blurted out, "They call me Ken." And then his mouth dropped open; he was surprised at himself for not being able to follow his own plan.

"And tell me, who are your parents, Ken?" Kadann demanded. "That is, if you even know." The Supreme Prophet gave an evil grin.

"I never knew my parents," Ken replied. "And even if I did, I wouldn't tell you their names."

"So that's your attitude, is it?" Kadann said sarcastically. "You still find it within you to resist—at least for the moment. But give it time, give it time . . ."

Kadann looked into Ken's eyes with a hypnotic stare, knitting his dark eyebrows together. "Now I'll ask you again. What do you know of your parents?"

"I—I think maybe my name Ken comes from Kenobi," he replied. "I think I may be the son of Obi-Wan Kenobi, but I can't prove it."

Kadann cleared his throat. "So that's what you think, is it? Quite a fantasy—that you might turn out to be a mysterious son of Obi-Wan Kenobi. You who grew up deep underground, raised by droids in the Lost City of the Jedi. And you probably think that's why they call you a Jedi Prince?" Kadann laughed a bitter laugh. "It might interest you to know that that's where we're heading—to the fourth moon of Yavin, and then to Lost City."

"You'll never find it without our help," Luke interrupted. "And we'll never help you."

"You've already helped me, Skywalker," Kadann said with a sneer. "You took Triclops to SPIN head-quarters, and he found the coordinates of the Lost City in one of your files. You didn't know that Triclops was an Imperial mole—one of our spies planted within your beloved Alliance. He's been in frequent communication with us, thanks to one of these—" Kadann held up a small round device, an implant like the one the Empire had inserted in Triclops's molar.

Luke and Ken exchanged a knowing glance. Was the plan working? Triclops had provided Kadann with disinformation about the location of the Lost City. However, it certainly appeared that Kadann believed the false coordinates to be accurate.

Luke and Ken were then led by the Imperials down a long hallway. Soon they reached an observation room with a huge window. There they were to remain under armed guard, and under the close, watchful gaze of several of the Imperial prophets.

Luke tried to concentrate on the Force. He realized that, using the power of the Jedi, he might be able to free his hands by moving the tumblers of the lock that held his wrists fastened behind his back. But try as he might, Luke was still unable to put himself in tune with the Force. His mind was cloudy, and his arms and legs still tingled from the effects of the stun-beam.

Soon the Imperial spaceship was hovering over Yavin Four, close to the location of the decoy entrance to the Lost City. Kadann entered the observation room. He then turned to High Prophet Jedgar and said, "It has occurred to me, Jedgar, that the information about how to find the Lost City came to me rather easily—suspiciously easily, I now realize. I'm going to send some stormtroopers into the jungle first. They're to fly in a command speeder, taking Grand Moff Hissa with them."

"Certainly, Kadann," Jedgar replied.

"Hissa should be the first to descend in the tubular transport to the Lost City," Kadann continued. "If this is a trick and he dies, nothing is lost, since he's been sentenced to death anyway."

Luke and Ken watched on a remote viewing screen. They saw stormtroopers take Grand Moff Hissa, who was still chained to his hover-chair, into the Imperial command speeder. They then descended to the jungle and landed. The screen showed Hissa being removed from the smaller spacecraft. His face wore a bitter scowl, the look of a soldier who had long served the Empire and now felt betrayed by the new Imperial leader.

The landing party continued until they reached the circular green marble wall. The door of the tubular transport opened, and the stormtroopers put Grand Moff Hissa, who was chained so that he could not escape, inside the transport. Then they programmed the controls for it to descend.

Kadann's inquisitive eyes were fixed on the screen too. He could see the tubular transport traveling deep underground.

Then the transport came to a stop. Hissa's chair, which had been designed to float only a few feet above the ground, went out of control as he steered it through the tubular transport door and over a gigantic hole. Hissa plunged, tumbling treacherously toward the volcanic river below. When he struck the flaming lava, he bobbed up and down, baked by the deadly molten sea.

"No, Kadann, noooooo!" Hissa screamed. But soon he melted into the fiery underground stream, and his charred remains sunk to its depths.

"So!" Kadann said with quiet fury. "The information I received from Triclops was a trick after all. You fed him false data, Luke Skywalker, hoping that it would lead me to my doom." Kadann bared his teeth and grunted. "Skywalker, you shall be the next to go down in that tubular transport to meet your death—that is, unless the Jedi Prince here cooperates and decides to tell me how to find the *real* entrance to the Lost City of the Jedi!"

"Don't help him, Ken," Luke said. "He's going to kill us anyway."

"Not true," Kadann retorted. "If you cooperate, Ken, you have my word that I'll set you both loose on the ice-world of Hoth. You'll have a sporting chance to survive. And the Supreme Prophet of the Dark Side never breaks his word of honor."

"Listen to what I'm telling you, Ken!" Luke said

firmly. "Whatever happens, don't help Kadann! Remember his prophecy: *'When the Jedi Knight becomes a captive of Scardia, then shall the Jedi Prince betray the Lost City.'*"

Kadann reached forward and touched Ken's birthstone. "I think you're about to join us, Ken," Kadann said. Then he turned toward the tall, dark prophet at his side. "Jedgar, take Luke Skywalker away!"

Kadann's order was promptly obeyed by Jedgar and several stormtroopers. Ken craned his neck to catch a last glimpse of Luke being led through a doorway and down a long corridor.

Luke refused to be led away without a fight, though he had nothing to fight with but his feet. He leaped and kicked a stormtrooper in the helmet, knocking him over. Then he tried the same tactic on High Prophet Jedgar, but the tall prophet caught Luke's boot before it struck him. Jedgar twisted it and sent the Jedi Knight plunging to the cold, hard floor.

Ken winced. Luke was in dire peril, and there was nothing Ken could do to help him.

Kadann slowly walked over to a case filled with valuable ornaments and relics. Opening the case, he removed a small piece of crystal, a half sphere.

At Kadann's request, Ken's hands were freed. Then Kadann offered Ken the piece of crystal he had removed from the case. "This is the other half of your birthstone," Kadann explained. "I got it from your father. It fits with the piece around your neck."

Ken quickly discovered that the two pieces fit

together perfectly. His mouth fell open in astonishment, and his mind was filled with wonder. How was this possible? Why would Kadann have the other half of his birthstone?

"I know all the secrets of your life that are unknown to you, Ken," Kadann said. "I know who brought you to the Lost City of the Jedi. And I know who your father is—and your grandfather. When you take me to the Lost City, Ken, I shall reveal to you *everything* about who you are. For the first time in your life, young Jedi Prince, you'll have the chance to learn where you came from—and your destiny!"

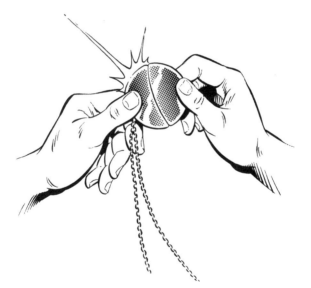

CHAPTER 6
Ken's Destiny

The temptation for Ken to cooperate with Kadann was becoming slowly overwhelming. Due to the few gulps of avabush spice tea Ken had swallowed, his judgment and his thinking were not as clear as they ordinarily were.

"You will tell me the location of the Lost City, Ken," Kadann said, staring at the boy intensely. Ken slowly felt his hatred of Kadann weakening, melting away.

Ken seriously considered telling Kadann what he wanted to know, because then Ken would learn the secrets about his origins—secrets that Dee-Jay and the other droids of the Lost City had always refused to reveal to him. Also, it would mean that Luke's life and his own life would be spared. Kadann had given his word that he would free them on the ice-world of Hoth, if Ken revealed the correct geographical coordinates of the Lost City.

Ken knew that Luke had once braved the bitter, icy weather of Hoth after Han Solo slayed a Taun Taun and covered Luke with its fur. Perhaps Ken and Luke could survive there until they were rescued by the Alliance.

Ken couldn't think straight. Although he knew

better, he yielded and gave Kadann the information that the Supreme Prophet of the Dark Side sought.

Kadann reacted swiftly. He instantly instructed the spaceship navigators where to go.

Ken was still in a daze. Soon the *Scardia Voyager* set down in the Yavin Four rain forest, not far from the site of the tubular transport that led directly underground to the Lost City.

The door of the spaceship was flung open. While Luke was kept prisoner aboard the *Scardia Voyager* on the ground, Ken found himself leading a large group. Following Ken on a route through the forest that Ken knew by heart were Kadann, High Prophet Jedgar, Prophet Gornash, an Imperial intelligence agent who was an expert at computers, and a group of stormtroopers. Kadann had left instructions that if there was any further trickery, Luke Skywalker was to be destroyed at once.

Once the Imperials and Ken were aboard the tubular transport, it descended swiftly, far into the ground.

When its door eventually slid open again, Kadann, realizing that no one could stop him now from reaching his goal, peered out at the cavern of the Lost City. For the first time he viewed with awe the many dome-houses and winding streets filled with caretaker droids at work.

Ken and the Imperials marched down a street made from green marble. When they passed Ken's dome-house at 12 South Jedi Lane, where Ken used to live, Zeebo the mooka leaped out of a window and came running up to Ken, jumping into his arms and lapping his face. Ken hugged his furry, feathery pet as hard as he could. Ken then suddenly felt a strange sensation, as though he were just beginning to wake up to what he had done.

"Put the animal down," Kadann commanded.

Zeebo suddenly leaped from Ken's arms and attacked Kadann, snapping and biting at him. Kadann tossed the mooka to the ground and kicked the alien animal. "Ksssshhhhh," Zeebo moaned, limping away as a stormtrooper followed after him.

"Leave Zeebo alone!" Ken shouted.

But the stormtrooper pulled out a stun-blaster and fired a stun-beam at Ken's pet. Zeebo suddenly became motionless.

"What have you done to him? You monsters!" Ken screamed.

Ken tried to run toward Zeebo, but two stormtroopers stopped him, grabbing Ken by the arms. The Jedi Prince struggled, but they dragged him along, following Kadann in the march over to North Jedi Lane.

When they arrived at the Jedi Library, the forces of Kadann entered the hallowed building. The hard boots of the stormtroopers stomped across the sleek, shiny floor, leaving behind ugly scrape marks.

Ken's eyes fell upon Dee-Jay, who was seated in a corner of the room near a case containing glittering relics of the Jedi Knights.

"Ken? What—Why did you lead them here?" Dee-Jay asked, his ruby-red eyes shining as he stared at the boy he had dutifully raised. "Why have you led the Empire to the most sacred place of the Jedi Knights?"

Ken's eyes grew moist as he searched for an answer. "I had to, Dee-Jay! They would have killed Luke if I had refused."

"Silence!" Kadann ordered. Then he turned to the tall, ancient droid. "You knew this day would come, didn't you, Dee-Jay?" Kadann said. "You've studied all of my prophecies."

Dee-Jay nodded. "Yes, I studied them. But I concluded that your prophecies about the Lost City of the Jedi had almost no probability of coming true."

Kadann spoke in a faraway-sounding, deep and mystical voice:

"When the Jedi Knight
Becomes a captive of Scardia,
Then shall the Jedi Prince

Betray the Lost City."

Kadann then turned to the Imperial intelligence agent. "Activate the computer!"

In a moment the computer was on-line, its menu of Jedi lore and knowledge filling the central screen. Kadann spent a few silent moments studying the blueprints of several Rebel Alliance fortresses, including DRAPAC, the Defense Research and Planetary Assistance Center located atop Mount Yoda on the planet Dagobah.

"Your most protected installations shall soon suffer an Imperial assault—an assault more powerful and effective than any we have launched against you before," Kadann declared. "It will mean the end of the Rebel Alliance once and for all—in one fiery explosion!" Then Kadann turned to Ken. "And now," he said, "it is time for you to learn the true secret of your parentage."

"Now you'll understand, Ken," Dee-Jay explained, "why all of us droids in this Jedi city believed you should never be told the truth about who you are until you became a grown man—old enough to accept the truth." Dee-Jay's ruby eyes grew dimmer as he fell into silence.

Kadann turned to Ken. "Though you were born with the blood of a Jedi," he explained, "your hunch that Obi-Wan Kenobi is your father is quite mistaken. You are no relation of Obi-Wan Kenobi. You are named Ken after your mother." Kadann glanced at the intelligence agent, narrowing his eyes to mere slits. "Call up the file on Kendalina."

In a moment, Ken saw the face of a beautiful, dark-haired woman on the computer screen.

"Kendalina was a Jedi Princess who was captured by Imperials," Kadann explained. "She was forced to pledge allegiance to the Empire, and she was assigned to work for many years as an Imperial nurse on the planet Kessel, deep in the spice mines."

Now the screen showed a picture of the building in the spice mines where Kendalina worked: The Imperial Insane Asylum of Kessel.

"That's where she met the man who became your father, Ken," Dee-Jay interrupted. "He was an Imperial prisoner, considered insane because he said he was a pacifist who believed in disarmament instead of war. He has three eyes. Two at the front of his head. One at the back."

"This is your father—" Kadann revealed.

Suddenly the screen showed a portrait of Triclops!

Ken felt his heart skip several beats as his throat constricted.

"You inherited many of your mother's features, Ken," Dee-Jay explained. "You have a natural talent for the Jedi arts and skills, like she did. You have her brown hair and her eyes. Fortunately, you didn't inherit your father's gene for a third eye, and you weren't born a mutant like he was. Now you know that you really do have Jedi blood in your veins—but you are also descended from the royal blood of the Empire!"

Ken's arms, limp and drained of all strength,

dropped to his sides.

"Behold—your grandfather!" Kadann declared.

On the screen Ken saw the image of Emperor Palpatine, sitting on a throne in the Death Star, the Emperor's face looking twisted, tortured, and evil.

"It can't be true!" Ken exclaimed. "Please, no, it isn't true!"

Losing control of his emotions, Ken struck the old, metal droid, pounding on Dee-Jay's chest and screaming out, "No, no . . ."

Dee-Jay calmly gripped Ken's wrists, saying sternly, "Be still! Why do you think you were brought to us, Ken? Because your mother wanted you to have a chance to overcome your grandfather's ways of darkness and evil. That's why we were chosen to raise you," Dee-Jay explained, "so that, under the guidance and teaching of the caretaker droids of the Lost City, your Jedi heritage could win out over the Dark Side that is also a part of your heritage."

"I've heard enough from that droid," Kadann declared. "Deactivate him!"

"Nooooo!" Ken screamed.

But the Imperial intelligence agent opened a panel in Dee-Jay's back and swiftly deactivated him, leaving the old droid motionless and silent.

Miles above, on the surface of Yavin Four, Luke Skywalker, who was being held under armed guard in a chamber aboard the *Scardia Voyager*, finally felt that the effects of the stun-beam had worn off. Himself once again, Luke sensed a disturbance in the Force.

The disturbance seemed to be coming from deep within the fourth moon of Yavin. It was a terrible feeling, a gnawing sensation that hinted at catastrophe for the Lost City. Then, as he closed his eyes and concentrated deeply, Luke intuitively realized that his sister, Princess Leia, was nearby. Surely that meant that an Alliance rescue mission was approaching.

Now that the stun-beam had worn off, Luke knew that the time had come for him to make his move. The first step was to free his hands from the Imperial wrist-cuffs that bound him. It took a little longer than usual, but Luke was able to put himself in total harmony with the Force, focusing his concentration on the metal lock at his wrists. Slowly the metal parts within the lock began to move.

CLIIIICK!

His hands were free! Luke concentrated now on clouding the minds of his captors.

"You lazy fools," Luke said to the armed guards. "Where is my tea that I asked for half an hour ago?"

"What tea?" the stormtrooper in charge asked.

"When Kadann asks for tea, he expects tea!" Luke demanded, using the old Jedi mind trick that his master Obi-Wan Kenobi had taught him. "Do you think the Supreme Prophet of the Dark Side likes to be kept waiting?"

"Of course not, Kadann," the stormtrooper apologized. He then turned to a companion. "How come you haven't brought Kadann his tea?"

It was working! Luke pushed harder, clouding the minds of every guard in the room and placing them in a state of extreme mental confusion.

"Never mind, I'll get it myself," Luke said. "Open the door and stay here."

"Yes, Kadann!" the stormtrooper in charge replied.

As the door was unlocked for him, Luke sensed that something was luring him toward a room three doors down the cold, gray hallway. Was danger awaiting him from that room? He quieted his mind and discovered that it was a sensation of attraction, not repulsion. He had nothing to fear from whatever was inside.

Quietly and quickly, Luke slid open the door. There his eyes were greeted by display cases containing some of Kadann's most priceless captured relics. And in the center was a new addition to this little museum of valuables. The sign above the display case read: LUKE SKYWALKER'S LIGHTSABER. And then, in smaller letters: THIS IS THE LIGHTSABER THAT CUT OFF THE RIGHT HAND OF DARTH VADER INSIDE THE IMPERIAL DEATH STAR.

Luke reached out his hand, beckoning the lightsaber to come toward him, just as he had once done on the ice-planet Hoth inside the cave of a Wampa creature.

The lightsaber rattled on its small stand, then struck the inside of the glass case, splintering it. As Luke concentrated even harder, the lightsaber once again smashed against the glass, then flew past the sharp jagged edges of broken glass and zoomed toward his outstretched hand. Drawn toward him by a mysterious mental magnetic attraction that only a Jedi Knight could understand, the lightsaber was soon in his grasp.

Luke turned it on, its glowing green blade stretching outward to defend him. Then Luke reentered the hall and crouched behind the large, rectangular engine-cooling module. He glanced toward the rear of the *Scardia Voyager*, certain that the Alliance assault would come in any second from that direction.

Luke was right! A Rebel Alliance assault team moved a garrison of equipment into position, creating an ion force field to shield themselves against the weapons of the *Scardia Voyager*. Led by Alliance leader Mon Mothma, and Han Solo, Chewbacca, Princess Leia, See-Threepio, and Artoo-Detoo, the Rebels used a captured Imperial TNT—a treaded neutron torch to punch a gaping hole in the aft of the golden Imperial spaceship. Then the Alliance staged a lightning charge.

Luke joined the action, working his way through the *Scardia Voyager*, using his lightsaber to swiftly defeat every stormtrooper who stood in his way. The Prophets of the Dark Side on board were quickly overpowered.

"Luke, that's the last time we send you out after macaab mushrooms," Han said, when they were safely outside the ship. "That was supposed to be a quick and easy trip, remember?"

"How did you find me?" Luke asked, giving his sister Leia a hug.

"A rather simple computation," the familiar voice of See-Threepio chimed in, as the golden droid came over to greet his master. "Artoo and I freed Chewbacca from the tentacle-bush after you and Ken were captured. Chewbacca then flew us back from that mushroom planet. We watched as the Imperial command speeder took you to the *Scardia Voyager*, and we continued tracking you all the way to Yavin Four, sending the coordinates on your flight movements back to SPIN!"

"Groooaaawwwwf!" Chewbacca moaned, congratulating himself on his contribution to their valiant rescue.

"*BdoobzOOOp!*" Artoo-Detoo added, popping out from behind the captured Imperial TNT. He spun his dome back and forth, demonstrating his enthusiasm at seeing Luke.

"Excellent work, Chewie—and you droids did a good job too!" Luke exclaimed. "But our work isn't finished yet. Kadann has gone down into the Lost City of the Jedi, and he has Ken hostage!"

Luke led his friends to the nearby green, circular marble wall. He attempted to operate the tubular transport, trying to make it depart from down in the Lost City and come to the surface again. But the controls didn't respond.

"At this rate, we'll never get down there to rescue Ken," Han Solo said.

"I have an idea!" Luke exclaimed. They hurried back to the captured Imperial TNT. Luke climbed inside, searching. Finally he came out, holding a long gray canister. He opened it, revealing a protective outfit that was designed as a heat shield. It even included a helmet. "Han, the climate of this planet is controlled by steam vents, remember? Those vents go from down in the Lost City all the way up to the surface. If I can't get down the tubular transport, then I'll slide down a steam vent—wearing this!" Luke held up the heat-resistant clothing. "I'll end up in the Lost City, at the Weather and Climate Control Center," Luke added excitedly.

"Sounds crazy to me," Han said.

"Totally crazy," Princess Leia agreed.

"But it's our only hope," Luke replied confidently. "We don't have any other choice!"

With help from Artoo-Detoo, whose heat sensors could detect steam from far away, they located the nearest steam vent deep in the jungle. Then they removed the grating that covered it.

When Luke peered down into the endless hole, he started to have second thoughts about his plan. He knew that Hologram Fun World had a ride through a black tube that twisted its way through a mile of darkness. But scary as that ride was, it was more like a slide. However, Luke realized that *this* ride would be more like a tumbling fall—and straight down for most of the way, with only the clouds of rising, hot steam to slow his descent!

Luke didn't want to go through with it. But then he thought of Ken. And a moment later, he closed his eyes, held his breath, and made the leap!

When Luke opened his eyes, he couldn't see the steam, but he could feel and hear it through his heat-protection outfit. The steam hissed and pushed against

him like a blast of scalding air, as he plunged into the endless darkness.

* * *

"You have great potential in the Dark Side, Ken," Kadann said to the boy, as Ken stared sadly at Dee-Jay's darkened eyes. "I can see that now. The Supreme Prophet of the Dark Side can never be wrong. But perhaps once . . . just once . . . I did make an error. That was when I urged Trioculus to find and destroy you. I know now that through your blood—the blood of Emperor Palpatine—you will one day lead the future generations of the Empire!"

"Never!" Ken declared firmly.

"Seize him!" Kadann ordered, gesturing to two stormtroopers who promptly overpowered Ken. They took Ken out of the Jedi Library and dragged him up the path as he kicked and struggled.

Kadann turned to his intelligence agent. "Is it

possible to remove the data files?"

"Removing the data chips from the master computer would destroy the Jedi files and all the information they contain."

"Then lift the master computer itself and take it to the tubular transport," Kadann ordered. "With that computer relocated to Space Station Scardia, all of the secrets of the Jedi will then belong to me!"

Kadann's stormtroopers prepared to transport the computer on a large, floating antigravity cart.

"Shut this city down," Kadann hissed. "Its final hour has come at last."

The Imperials departed from the library and headed back toward the tubular transport, deactivating everything in sight, silencing every last droid and machine of the Lost City. With every street Kadann passed, the lights went out, and the cavern dimmed a little more.

Suddenly Kadann was startled to see the Jedi Knight, Luke Skywalker, standing in the path, blocking their way. How was this possible, Kadann wondered, when Luke was Kadann's prisoner on board the *Scardia Voyager*?

"Let the boy go, Kadann," Luke said, brandishing his lightsaber.

"Luke!" Ken screamed.

Kadann took a few steps backward as the blade swung toward him. The stormtroopers who were holding Ken stepped back too, as Ken struggled to loosen himself from their grasp.

"I said let the boy go!" Luke repeated. "Now!"

Kadann was startled, not understanding how Luke could have possibly reached the Lost City. The tubular transport had remained at the bottom of the shaft ever since Kadann had arrived.

Just then Luke charged a group of stormtroopers, freeing Ken and taking the boy with him. As they ran, Ken spotted his stunned pet, Zeebo the mooka. Ken stopped just long enough to pick Zeebo up and carry him off. Laserfire from portable Imperial laser cannons streaked past Luke and Ken, as they swiftly slipped away toward the tubular transport.

"Master," Prophet Gornash called out to Kadann, "all that matters is the Jedi computer. Let's forget the Rebels for now and take it to the tubular transport, and depart!"

But as the computer was moved, one of the stormtroopers, firing his portable laser cannon after Ken and Luke, accidentally let loose with a blast that zoomed right toward Kadann.

Kadann moved quickly out of the path of danger. The laserblast struck the master Jedi computer instead, imploding the data screen and melting the main controls.

"Noooo!" Kadann shouted.

Meanwhile the stormtroopers continued to shut down the power in the Lost City, which became darker and darker.

Soon the only light remaining came from streaks of random laserfire, and the glow from inside the tubular transport as it began traveling toward the surface with Luke, Ken, and Zeebo safely inside.

CHAPTER 7
The Red Carpet

For a moment Luke and Ken were silent, and the only noise was the sound of the tubular transport rising at an incredibly fast speed. Then Ken spoke.

"Triclops is my father, Luke," Ken said in dismay. "I know it now."

"How do you know that?" Luke asked in a shocked but calm, steady voice.

"Kadann used the Jedi computer to show me my mother and father," Ken explained. "This means I'm also the grandson of Emperor Palpatine. Dee-Jay knew the secret all along, and he never told me!" The boy paused to choke down his tears. "So now you know the terrible truth. You now know where I come from—from evil."

"You're forgetting that my father was Darth Vader," Luke replied, staring into Ken's troubled eyes. "He too was devoted to evil. But the good in him survived deep within his heart, and at the very end of his life, it won out."

"All this time I thought . . . I hoped that my father would turn out to be Obi-Wan Kenobi," Ken said, glancing down. "But instead—this is the worst news I could have heard, Luke. I don't deserve to be part of the Rebel Alliance."

"The fact that my father chose a path of evil is no reflection on me," Luke explained. "It doesn't mean that I'm any less of a person, or any less of a man. Unlike my father, I proved myself strong enough to resist the lure of the Dark Side. And you've got to prove yourself strong enough to do the same too."

"And what if I'm not strong enough?" Ken asked.

"You will be," Luke replied. "Ken, no one is responsible for who their parents are. Or their grandparents. The choices they made in their lives are their own. But the choices we make are *our* own. We can't blame ourselves for the evil that our parents and grandparents did—only for what *we* do. And so it's up to each of us to make the right choices in life, to trust in the Force, and become the person that we know we should be."

Ken could feel Zeebo's little heart thumping as he held his four-eared pet in his arms. The speed of the tubular transport was awesome. Ken felt as if his stomach had been left far below, and he tingled from his ears to his toes.

But suddenly the tubular transport started to vibrate furiously. Then it slowed to a dead stop halfway up the elevator shaft.

The power had failed. They were trapped.

At the Senate building on Yavin Four, before Triclops could be given the special chemical made from the macaab mushroom, something strange overcame him. Triclops sat down to write a letter, but when he was done, he suddenly changed from a passive and gentle person to an angry maniac with superhuman strength.

Triclops's guards were in shock as he demonstrated an awesome power—a power they had never seen before. He tore their laser pistols from their hands, crushed the weapons, and picked the guards up and hurled them, smashing them against the laboratory wall.

Then Triclops bent the bars of two security doors and forced his way through them.

The tubular transport hadn't moved another inch, and Luke, Ken, and Zeebo were still surrounded by darkness, unable to escape.

"Ksssshhhhhh," Zeebo whined timidly. "Ksssh?"

"Uh-oh," Ken said despondently. "Looks like we're history."

"Aren't you forgetting something, Ken?" Luke asked, putting a hand on the young Jedi Prince's shoulder.

"Like what?"

"The Force. With trust in the Force, we can do *anything*," Luke said. "Even move tons of solid steel. Once I watched Yoda use the Force to lift my spaceship out of the swamps of Dagobah—it floated, weightless, until he set it down. The Force is a Jedi's strength, Ken. The Force is the power that flows through all things, the power behind the light of the stars—"

In the darkness, Luke began to banish all other thoughts from his mind, putting himself in total harmony with the Force, letting its power and energy flow through him. He breathed slowly, evenly, forgetting about the rising and falling of his chest, the inhales, the exhales. Only one thought remained in his mind—the wonder of the Force.

Suddenly there was a brief jolt, and the transport rose several inches. A few seconds passed. Then came a slow, gliding movement upward, as the power of the Force helped the transport move several feet farther. There was about a mile left to go.

"Help me, Ken," Luke said. "Empty your mind . . . feel the Force."

Ken tried to banish his fears and all other thoughts from his mind.

"Kshshshshshsh," Zeebo moaned, trembling in Ken's arms. Ken knew that this tubular transport was like a deep underground coffin. If it never moved again, the transport would become their tomb—in a million years, some explorer might find this elevator shaft and discover their remains.

But Ken knew he had to stop thinking about that. He knew he had to have positive thoughts—thoughts of life, not death.

"Only the Force, Ken," Luke said. "Keep your whole mind, your entire being, focused on the Force."

Suddenly the tubular transport began to move. It ascended slowly at first, and then it accelerated, going faster and faster as it continued to rise inside the elevator shaft—powered only by the pure energy of the Force.

When the tubular transport finally arrived Topworld, its door slid open, and dazzling green light filtered through the leaves of the rain forest and reflected brightly in their eyes. As their eyes adjusted to the sunlight, Luke, Ken, and Zeebo slowly stepped outside the transport and into the rain forest.

It wasn't long before Luke and Ken were reunited with the Rebel Alliance members of SPIN who had laid seige to the *Scardia Voyager*. The reunion included Princess Leia, Han Solo, and Chewbacca, as well as the droids, See-Threepio and Artoo-Detoo.

"Well, at last it seems that we're all one big happy family once again," Threepio said cheerfully. "That is, if the word *family* isn't reserved for only humans and can be expanded to include droids."

"Of course you're part of our family, Threepio," Luke said with a smile. "And Wookiees are part of our family, too—right, Chewie?"

"Awwwooooooo!" Chewbacca howled happily.

"Kshshshshhhh," Zeebo purred, as if wanting mookas to be included as well.

Although they were all greatly relieved, there was little time for celebration. One major problem remained which concerned them more than any other. Kadann was still down in the Lost City. But could they keep him down there? Perhaps—if the tubular transport was shut down permanently. Then Kadann would be cut off from his Prophets of the Dark Side who were still stationed back at the cube-shaped Space Station Scardia. Unable to come Topworld, Kadann would no longer be able to threaten the Alliance.

"We could remove the control mechanism of the tubular transport," Princess Leia suggested. "That would prevent Kadann from ever escaping."

"Don't forget, Princess, there are steam vents from the Lost City that reach the surface at many different locations on this moon," Luke replied. "Since I was able to reach the Lost City by sliding down a steam vent, Kadann could perhaps find some way to rise up to the surface through one of them. Besides, Prophets Gornash, Jedgar, and other Imperials are still down there with him. They could help him. There are also documents in the Jedi Library he'll be able to study and learn from. If he ever returns, he'll surely be an even stronger enemy."

"At least he's trapped for the moment," Leia said. "Our best hope for now is to shut down the tubular transport up here at the top of the shaft."

Upon hearing Leia's words, Ken felt a pang of sadness. He would never see Dee-Jay or return home again, he realized. His past was behind him, and he could never go back. He was now completely on his own.

As he watched Luke and Leia remove the control mechanism of the tubular transport, Ken wondered whether Triclops knew that he was his son.

When Ken returned to the Alliance Senate building, he quickly discovered that he wouldn't be able to confront his father after all. Ken wanted to talk with Triclops, to tell him he knew the truth. But Triclops was gone. The last anyone had seen of him was when he escaped into the rain forest, his third eye staring out the back of his head at the SPIN troops who tried in vain to go after the prisoner and capture him.

But Ken's father had left something behind—a personal letter with Ken's name on the envelope. Ken's hands trembled as he opened the letter to read it.

Dear Ken,

I've missed you ever since you were taken from me and sent to live with the droids in the Lost City of the Jedi. I've known since the day you and Luke rescued me back on Duro that you are my son. I knew by the birth crystal you wore.

I know what a shock it must have been for you to realize that your grandfather was Emperor Palpatine. And the things I must do in the days ahead will surely shock you just as much. All I can say is, do not believe all the terrible things you will hear about me.

Trust in me. And if the day comes when you can
no longer have faith in me, then trust in the Force,
as your Jedi mother Kendalina did. Perhaps then you
will discover that there is goodness in my heart.
   Until we meet again,
      Your loving father,
         Triclops

Ken kept the contents of the letter a secret. He told Luke he would share it with him someday, but he wasn't ready yet to show it to anyone. It was a personal message meant just for him—his last link with his father, who had gone off mysteriously, perhaps never to be seen again.

But Ken refused to give up hope that his father might one day be found. Without a spaceship, Triclops would have no way to depart from the fourth moon of Yavin. Ken asked Luke if SPIN could organize a search party, to try to track his father deep into the jungle.

"I'm sure Mon Mothma will agree to that," Luke said. "But there are hundreds of caves and thickets here in the rain forest where Triclops could hide and never be detected for years and years. In the meantime, there are other things we must worry about, Ken," Luke continued, "such as getting ready for Leia and Han's big day!"

Before Ken knew it, that eagerly awaited day had arrived. It was a very special day for Luke too, for he would be giving his sister's hand in marriage to his good friend, Han Solo.

To Luke, the wedding day seemed very much like the festive day of celebration they once had after the explosion of the first Imperial Death Star. The location was the same, and all the guests seemed filled with joy as they stood on both sides of the red wedding carpet on the path that led to the Senate entrance. Dignitaries who had arrived from many planets throughout the galaxy were waiting excitedly for the formal ceremony to be commenced by Mon Mothma.

Standing at the far end of the red carpet, Princess Leia, who was holding her wedding bouquet, looked over at Luke and smiled at him. She then glanced around and saw Ken and all her other friends.

Chewbacca was on hand to serve as Han's Best Man. And See-Threepio and Artoo-Detoo were there to share the title of Best Droid, both of them showing off their gleaming polish.

In the moments before it would be time for her to walk up the carpet and say "I do," Leia calmly put herself in tune with the Force. And for an instant she thought she had a vision of the future.

It was a glimpse of a time to come—a time when Leia would live with Han peacefully and safely in his sky house, floating in the air near Cloud City. It was also a time after their children had already been born.

Leia saw Han sitting with their children—there were two of them, one on each knee—as Han told the kids stories about his adventures flying the *Millen-*

nium Falcon in the days of the great battles against the evil Empire.

Would their children be twins? Taking a quick breath, Leia wondered if she and Han could possibly handle twins. She struggled to glimpse the hazy vision more clearly, to see whether their children were to be boys or girls—or a boy and a girl? But her vision vanished before the answer came to her.

Leia nodded to herself, ready to accept whatever was to come her way. She then stared at the long red carpet that made a path between her and the altar.

Enjoying the scent of her bouquet of bright flowers, Leia glanced over at her brother Luke, and exchanged another smile. Then she turned her gaze toward Han, her husband-to-be. He looked at her adoringly in return and smiled, as she prepared to take her first steps down the aisle.

Glossary

Arachnor
A giant spiderlike creature that spins very sticky webs, found on the planet Arzid.

Avabush spice
A truth serum from the spice mines of Kessel. Frequently served in tea or baked into biscuits, avabush spice may also bring on sleepiness.

Bnach
Scorching, cracked world where Imperial prisoners work in rock quarries.

Cloud City
A floating city above the planet Bespin that used to be a popular center of tourism, with its hotels and casinos. It is considered one of the galaxy's major trading posts, and the site of a Tibanna gas mining and exporting operation.

Dagobah Tech
The school that Ken attends on the planet Dagobah, run by the Rebel Alliance. His classmates are the sons and daughters of the scientists who work at DRAPAC, the Alliance fortress on Mount Yoda.

Dee-Jay (DJ-88)
A powerful caretaker droid and teacher in the Lost City of the Jedi. He is white, with eyes like rubies. His face is distinguished, with a metal beard. He is like a father to Ken,

having raised him from the time the young Jedi was a small child.

Defeen
A cunning, sharp-clawed Defel alien. Defeen has been promoted from interrogator first class at the Imperial Reprogramming Institute on the planet Duro to supreme interrogator for the Prophets of the Dark Side at Space Station Scardia.

Grand Moff Hissa
The Imperial grand moff (high-ranking Imperial governor) whom Trioculus trusted the most. He has spear-pointed teeth, and now rides in a hover-chair, having lost his arms and legs in a flood of liquid toxic waste on the planet Duro. His arms have been replaced with arms taken from an Imperial assassin droid.

HC-100 (Homework Correction Droid-100)
His appearance resembles that of See-Threepio, though he is silver in color, with blue eyes and a round mouth. HC-100 was designed by the droid Dee-Jay for the purpose of correcting and grading Ken's homework.

High Prophet Jedgar
A seven-foot-tall prophet whom Kadann, the Supreme Prophet of the Dark Side, most relies upon to help fulfill his prophecies and commands.

Hologram Fun World
Located inside a glowing, transparent dome floating in the center of a blue cloud of helium gas in outer space, Hologram Fun World is a theme park, where a "World of Dreams Come True" awaits every visitor. Lando Calrissian is now the Baron Administrator of the theme park.

Hoth
The frozen world where the Alliance once fought the four-legged Imperial AT-AT snow walkers. The Rebel Alliance deserted its base there; the ice planet is now the site of an Imperial base and prison.

Human Replica Droid
A lifelike droid designed in a secret Rebel Alliance lab at DRAPAC to look like a specific person. Its purpose is to act as a decoy and fool an enemy into thinking it's real. Human Replica Droids have eyes that can fire laser beams.

Imperial probe droid
A floating, robotic spy device that the Empire launches and sends to various planets in order to collect information about the Rebel Alliance.

Jabba the Hutt
A sluglike alien gangster and smuggler who owned a palace on Tatooine and consorted with alien bounty hunters. He was strangled to death by Princess Leia, choked by the chain that held her prisoner in his sail barge at the Great Pit of Carkoon.

Jawa
A meter-high creature who travels the deserts of Tatooine collecting and selling scrap. It has glowing orange eyes that peer out from under its hooded robe.

Jedi Library
A great library in the Lost City of the Jedi. The Jedi Library has records that date back thousands of years. Most of its records are in files in the Jedi master computer. Others are on ancient manuscripts and old, yellowed books. Gathered in this library is all the knowledge of all civilizations

and the history of all planets and moons that have intelligent life-forms.

Kadann
A black-bearded dwarf, Kadann is the Supreme Prophet of the Dark Side. He has now assumed the leadership of the Empire.

Ken
A twelve-year-old Jedi Prince who was raised by droids in the Lost City of the Jedi after being brought to the underground city as a small child by a Jedi Knight in a brown robe. He knows many Imperial secrets, which he learned from studying the files of the master Jedi computer in the Jedi Library where he went to school. Long an admirer of Luke Skywalker, he has departed the Lost City, joined the Alliance, and is now a student at Dagobah Tech on Mount Yoda on the planet Dagobah.

Kendalina
A Jedi Princess who was forced to serve as a nurse in an Imperial insane asylum deep in the spice mines of Kessel.

Lost City of the Jedi
An ancient, technologically advanced city built long ago by Jedi Knights. The city is located deep underground on the fourth moon of Yavin, where Ken, the Jedi Prince, was raised by droids.

Mon Mothma
A distinguished-looking leader, she has long been in charge of the Rebel Alliance.

Mount Yoda
A mountain on the planet Dagobah, named in honor of the late Jedi Master, Yoda. This is the site where the Rebel

Alliance built DRAPAC, their new Defense Research and Planetary Assistance Center.

Mouth of Sarlacc
The mouth of a giant, omnivorous, multitentacled beast at the bottom of the Great Pit of Carkoon on Tatooine, beyond the Dune Sea. Anyone who falls to the bottom of the pit will be swallowed by the Sarlacc and slowly digested over a period of one thousand years.

Omniprobe
Omniprobes are devices that can go after probe droids, targeting them for destruction. As a homework assignment in the Lost City of the Jedi, Ken designed a blueprint for an advanced Jedi Omniprobe, with considerable help from his droid-teacher, Dee-Jay.

Prophet Gornash
One of Kadann's prophets, he coordinates spy activities in Space Station Scardia.

Prophets of the Dark Side
A sort of Imperial Bureau of Investigation run by black-bearded prophets who work within a network of spies. The prophets have much power within the Empire. To retain their control, they make sure their prophecies come true—even if it takes bribery or murder.

Sandcrawler
A large transport vehicle used by the jawas.

Scardia Voyager
The gold-colored spaceship of the Prophets of the Dark Side.

Space Station Scardia
A cube-shaped space station where the Prophets of the Dark Side live.

SPIN
An acronym for the Senate Planetary Intelligence Network, a Rebel Alliance troubleshooting organization. All the major Star Wars Alliance heroes are members of SPIN, which has offices both on Yavin Four and at DRAPAC on Mount Yoda on the planet Dagobah.

Tatooine
A desert planet with twin suns, Tatooine is Luke Skywalker's home planet.

Tentacle-bush
A low-lying bush with octopuslike tentacles found on the mushroom planet, Arzid. Usually the tentacles snatch rodents for its food.

Topworld
An expression that refers to the surface of the fourth moon of Yavin. When the droids of the Lost City of the Jedi talk about going Topworld, they mean taking the tubular transport to the surface.

Triclops
The true mutant, three-eyed son of the late Emperor Palpatine. Triclops has spent most of his life in Imperial insane asylums, but is now under observation by the Alliance at DRAPAC. He has two eyes on the front of his head and one on the back. He has scars on his temples from shock treatments, and his hair is white and jagged, sticking out in all directions.

Trioculus

A three-eyed mutant who was the Supreme Slavelord of Kessel, and who later became Emperor. Trioculus was a liar and impostor who claimed to be the son of Emperor Palpatine. In his rise to power as Emperor, he was supported by the grand moffs, who helped him find the glove of Darth Vader, an everlasting symbol of evil.

Tubular transport

A transport device similar to an elevator that travels up and down a shaft through miles of rock. The tubular transport enables one to travel Topworld from the underground Lost City of the Jedi.

Yoda

The Jedi Master Yoda was a small creature who lived on the bog planet Dagobah. For eight hundred years before passing away he taught Jedi Knights, including Obi-Wan Kenobi and Luke Skywalker, in the ways of the Force.

Zeebo

Ken's four-eared alien pet mooka, he has both fur and feathers.

Zorba the Hutt

The father of Jabba the Hutt. A sluglike creature with a long braided white beard, Zorba was a prisoner on the planet Kip for over twenty years. He returned to Tatooine to discover that his son was killed by Princess Leia. He later became Governor of Cloud City by beating Lando Calrissian in a rigged card game of sabacc in the Holiday Towers Hotel and Casino.

PAUL DAVIDS, a graduate of Princeton University and the American Film Institute Center for Advanced Film Studies, has had a lifelong love of science fiction. He was the executive producer of and cowrote the film *Roswell* for Showtime. *Roswell* starred Kyle MacLachlan and Martin Sheen and was nominated for a Golden Globe for Best TV Motion Picture of 1994.

Paul was the production coordinator and a writer for the television series *The Transformers*. He is currently the producer and director of a documentary feature film titled *Timothy Leary's Dead*. His first book, *The Fires of Pele: Mark Twain's Legendary Lost Journal*, was written with his wife, Hollace, with whom he also wrote the six Skylark Star Wars novels. The Davids live in Los Angeles.

HOLLACE DAVIDS is Vice President of Special Projects at Universal Pictures. Her job includes planning and coordinating all the studio's premieres and working on the Academy Awards campaigns. Hollace has an A.B. in psychology, *cum laude*, from Goucher College and an Ed.M. in counseling psychology from Boston University. After teaching children with learning disabilities, Hollace began her career in the entertainment business by working for the Los Angeles International Film Exposition. She then became a publicist at Columbia Pictures, and seven years later was named Vice President of Special Projects at Columbia. She has also worked for TriStar Pictures and Sony Pictures Entertainment.

Whether it's because they grew up in nearby hometowns (Hollace is from Silver Spring, Maryland, and Paul is from Bethesda) or because they share many interests, collaboration comes naturally to Paul and Hollace Davids—both in their writing and in raising a family. The Davids have a daughter, Jordan, and a son, Scott.

About the Illustrators

JUNE BRIGMAN was born in 1960 in Atlanta, Georgia, and has been drawing since she was old enough to hold a pencil. She studied art at the University of Georgia and Georgia State University, but her illustrations are based on real-life observation and skills she developed over a summer as a pastel portrait artist at Six Flags Over Georgia amusement park, when she was only sixteen. At twenty she discovered comic books at a comic convention, and by the time she was twenty-two she got her first job working for Marvel Comics, where she created the *Power Pack* series. A devout horse enthusiast and Bruce Springsteen fan, Ms. Brigman lives and works in White Plains, New York.

KARL KESEL was born in 1959 and raised in the small town of Victor, New York. He started reading comic books at the age of ten, while traveling cross-country with his family, and decided soon after that he wanted to become a cartoonist. By the age of twenty-five, he landed a full-time job as an illustrator for DC Comics, working on such titles as *Superman, World's Finest, Newsboy Legion,* and *Hawk and Dove,* which he also cowrote. He was also one of the artists on the *Terminator* and *Indiana Jones* miniseries for Dark Horse Comics. Mr. Kesel lives and works with his wife, Barbara, in Milwaukie, Oregon.

DREW STRUZAN is a teacher, lecturer, and one of the most influential forces working in commercial art today. His strong visual sense and recognizable style have produced lasting pieces of art for advertising, the recording industry, and motion pictures. His paintings include the album covers for *Alice*

Cooper's Greatest Hits and *Welcome to My Nightmare,* which was recently voted one of the one hundred classic album covers of all time by *Rolling Stone* magazine. He has also created the movie posters for Star Wars, *E.T. the Extra-Terrestrial,* the Back to the Future series, the Indiana Jones series, *An American Tale,* and *Hook.* Mr. Struzan lives and works in the California valley with his wife, Cheryle. Their son, Christian, is continuing in the family tradition, working as an art director and illustrator.